A TOR DOUBLE ACTION WESTERN

Look for the Tor Double Action Westerns from these authors:

FRANK BONHAM
MAX BRAND
HARRY SINCLAIR DRAGO
CLAY FISHER
STEVE FRAZEE
ZANE GREY
WILL HENRY
WAYNE D. OVERHOLSER
LEWIS B. PATTEN
JOHN PRESCOTT
W.C. TUTTLE
OWEN WISTER

Norman A. Fox

HELL AND HOT LEAD

GUN-RIDER

TOR®
A TOM DOHERTY ASSOCIATES BOOK
NEW YORK

HELL AND HOT LEAD

GUN-RIDER

A Tor Book
Published by Tom Doherty Associates, Inc.
49 West 24th Street
New York, N.Y. 10010

Cover art by TK

ISBN: 0-812-51315-0

First edition: March 1991

Printed in the United States of America

0 9 8 7 6 5 4 3 2 1

HELL AND HOT LEAD

• Chapter 1 •

The wind, sighing dismally along Caprock's false-fronted street, swept down across the prairie with the teeth of winter in it. Yet the tall, leathery man who bucked it along the boardwalk was oblivious to the icy blast. He was a man whose thoughts had turned inward, as he strode toward the meeting hall on the cowtown's outskirts, who might be on his way to pronounce his own doom.

His name was Henry Harlow McGrath, but Montana knew him from the Marias to the Yellowstone as "Hellvation Hank" McGrath, a circuit-riding sky pilot who might christen a baby and thrash a bully all in the same morning, doing each chore with a zealot's thoroughness. A fighting preacher, this Hellvation Hank. Now there was a new battle for him, but it was not just another fight. Not when a man had to choose between loyalty to a friend and his duty as he saw it.

Yet his decision was made and Hellvation Hank shouldered purposefully into the meeting hall which was his church when he chose so to use it. The place was narrow and dark and benches served as pews while a raised platform with a table was the only altar. The room was packed and there was a restless stir at his entrance as though the excitement that gripped Caprock was concentrated here.

Excitement! It was only a shadow of things to come, McGrath reflected as he glimpsed Tyler Whitman in the congregation. Wherever Whitman was there'd be excitement, for he was president of Montana-Pacific, the roaring railroad that had pushed across the untamed Dakotas with the end of steel already nearing Caprock. There'd be a new boom in Caprock with grading contracts for those who wanted them, and beef contracts to supply the hungry crews with food. The town was a magnet to draw the reputable and the disreputable, the forces of good and the powers of evil.

The sky pilot, a bony man, gray-headed and looking older than his forty-odd years, took his place behind the table. He dragged a Bible from a cavernous pocket of his shapeless black coat, but did not open it. Instead he stood there with the Book in his hand, his face calm and emotionless.

"I'll use no text tonight," he announced. "It's not the Sabbath, and it's not a sermon I'm here to preach. I bring you a warning."

A gusty sigh rippled across his congregation and he waited.

"You are a happy people," he said then. "You know that a dream long cherished by most of us is to be realized. The railroad is coming to Caprock. We will see a boom while the end of steel is here and we'll see a more enduring prosperity afterward. Ranchers will be able to ship cattle to Eastern markets without losing the profit on the way. Mines will open in the Big Thunders and those mountains will surrender their riches. A day we have long awaited will come, a day I have prayed to see, since with it will come law and order. Our Eden is almost within reach. But like the Eden of old, it has its serpent. Our serpent is a three-headed one."

He paused, studying the faces before him, hearing the creak of benches, seeing neighbor stare covertly at neighbor.

"Three men," he said bluntly, "will stoop to any means to keep Montana-Pacific from crossing the Big Thunders. They are men who think only of themselves. Their names are known to me. Part of their plans are known to me. By the grace of God, I am sometimes His instrument of mercy. One fallen brother I cannot name told me of these three. The secret is mine."

There was a subtle change in his voice while a zealot's fire gave life to his bony face. "I do not say these three are here," he went on. "But my word will reach them. I give them one week to mend their ways. Let them come to me and prove their repentance and the matter shall be forever forgotten. If they choose, instead, to go on their sinful way, I shall have no choice. One week from tonight I shall stand here and expose them for what they are. Good night, my friends. May God go with you."

He was down from the platform before a man moved and, as was his custom, stationed himself at the door to shake each person's hand as he left. The first man out was gray-headed Thackery Weaver, editor of the Caprock *Tribune*. He was scribbling notes, so intent that he did not see McGrath's outstretched hand.

After the editor came Tyler Whitman, a soldierly man who looked uncomfortable in his white silk shirt and broadcloth. With him was sun-tanned, poker-faced Kurt Ormond, his chief construction engineer. The railroad builder took McGrath's hand.

"Sorry I've been so busy I haven't had time for a talk with you Hank," Whitman said. "The years have changed you, my friend. Who'd guess that twenty years ago we were both eating the dust of the drag down on the Brazos? And who'd think that I'd turn out to be a railroad builder and you a gospel shouter?''

''It's been a long time, Ty,'' said Hellvation Hank, the warmth of genuine affection in his smile.

Broad-shouldered ''Curly'' Bottsinger, owner of the stage and freight line in this wild country from the Dakota border to the Big Thunders, brushed past without a word, and after him came fancy-dressed Hoyt Durham, owner of the Golden Slipper Saloon. McGrath regarded him with surprise. ''Didn't expect to find you at church, Durham,'' he said.

Durham shrugged. ''Why not?'' he countered. ''I might as well close up my place any time you twist the devil's tail. Seems like you put on a better show than all my percentage girls who—''

It was not so much what he was saying but the way he was saying it that darkened McGrath's face with anger.

''Stop!'' he shouted. ''You can't mention foulness in the shadow of the House of God!''

''To hell I can't!'' Durham said, and spat toward the open doorway.

McGrath hit him then, his fist crashing against Durham's chin. His freshly lighted cigar showered sparks as it arced away while Durham sprawled backward upon the ground. He came to his feet with killer fury in his eyes but he contented himself with a barbed glance at the sky pilot.

''You'll pay for that some day, gospel-grinder!'' he said and stalked off.

Tyler Whitman frowned, but Kurt Ormond was as inscrutable as ever. Now another man was barging from the doorway, a semi-bald old cattleman who plucked at McGrath's sleeve while he crossed palms with Tyler Whitman.

''What the dickens is all the mystery about, Hank?'' the cowman demanded. ''What's this palaver about three side-winders? You meanin' me? You know dang well I'm ag'in the cast-iron cayuse that Ty, here, figgers he's goin' to run across this range. You think I want my Deadman range cluttered up with hoe-men? That's what the railroad will bring!"

McGrath considered Storm Herndon of the H-in-a-Hat spread with a good-natured smile.

"You're a long way off your range, *amigo*," he observed. "You wouldn't be in Caprock to angle for a railroad beef contract would you, Storm? How's that girl of yours?"

"Lana? She's kickin' over the traces again. Says she's through with Eastern schoolin'. Says she's comin' home next spring whether I like it or not."

Herndon bustled off then. The rest of the congregation paraded down Caprock's street until only Hank McGrath and the two railroad men stood there in the dusk.

"Those three men you mentioned, Hank," Tyler Whitman said. "I'd be mighty interested in knowing their names. Since the Government's promised to subsidize the first railroad to cross the Big Thunders, Central Western has been bucking me every step of the way and it's trouble enough putting the rails through. I've got ways of catching my own rats, Hank, but I'd like to know who you were driving at."

Hellvation Hank's leathery face clouded.

"Do you suppose I haven't thought of that, Ty?" he asked. "We're old friends, and those three are striking at the heart of the thing you're trying to do—the thing I want to see you succeed in doing, not for your sake or for mine, but for Montana's. Even when I was walking down here, I was deciding where my duty lay. But I've got my work too. I've got to save men from the wickedness within them. Even those three. They'll have their chance to redeem themselves."

"Maybe so," Whitman conceded drily. "But I've got a trouble-shooter, name of Dan Callishaw, who knows the right way of saving gents from their own wickedness. But I don't suppose we could see eye to eye on *that*. So long, pard."

They shook hands again, two old friends who had shared their formative years together before each had taken a different trail. Whitman strode away with Kurt Ormond, and the sky pilot bent his footsteps toward his isolated home.

In the clapboard shack beyond the town, the wind slipped through so that when McGrath lighted a kerosene lamp on the split-log table in the single room, the flame flickered wildly. The sky pilot busied himself at the stove, building a fire mechanically, for the magnitude of the challenge he'd made filled his thoughts.

Had he said too much? If there was fear within him, characteristically it wasn't for himself. But he was remembering the man who had first warned him of the three who threatened the Montana-Pacific Railroad. He hadn't intended to jeopardize the fellow.

While he was turning the matter over in his mind he heard a faint sound outside. It was no more than the scrape of a boot sole against the hard-packed earth but it brought McGrath to the door where he peered into the murk.

"Who is it?" he called, then recognized the silent figure a few paces away.

So short a time ago he had asked three men to come to him, and already one of them was here. To repent—or to take advantage? It was like Hellvation Hank to give the man the benefit of the doubt.

"My seed seems to have been cast upon fertile ground," he called. "Won't you come in, my friend?"

His answer came in blossoming gun-flame and the crash of a six-gun. Stunned by the tearing, burning impact of the slug, Hellvation Hank spun, teetering on his toes in the doorway for an endless moment before he fell full length upon the ground. And as he sprawled there, the assassin was already slipping away in the darkness.

There was blood on Hellvation Hank's fingers as he clutched his shattered chest and there was a great sadness in his heart—the sadness of Him who said: "Father, forgive them, for they know not what they do." But the fighting heart of Hellvation Hank had its say, too, and its voice was the voice of the anger that was raging in his heart.

He was dying. He had tended too many dying men not to know that his own hour had come. He had defied the evil forces threatening the coming of steel, and those forces had struck him down.

He had made a grave mistake in not giving their names to Tyler Whitman. Now he must warn his friend somehow, name the three, so that Tyler Whitman might guard against them.

There were writing materials in the shack but when he tried to crawl toward the doorway he found his strength was not enough.

He thought to scratch three names in the earth but the ground was hard-packed and defied his faltering fingers. He tried again to reach the doorway and succeeded only in working the Bible out of his pocket where it lay in the yellow splash of light, the cold evening wind fingering the worn old pages.

Looking at the Book, the light of inspiration glowed in the dimming eyes of Hellvation Hank. He flipped the pages he knew so well, turning unerringly to certain passages. These he marked with the only means at hand, smearing the passages with his own life blood.

And his task was finished before his fingers stiffened and his painwracked body lay still.

When morning came the first snow lay like a shroud, blanketing Caprock and the range beyond and sifting softly over the body of Hellvation Hank McGrath.

• Chapter 2 •

April smiled upon Caprock range. The rolling prairie, freed from icy fetters, moon-mellowed and alive with the first faint stirrings of spring, spread before the man from Texas who followed the twin rails toward the distant town.

The land that had belonged to the Kiowas, the Choctaws and the Chikasaws had known this lean young rider, and he had breasted the Red, the Brazos, the Washita and all those treacherous streams that intersect the north trail from Texas. He wore cowboy garb and something in his tanned face proved he had crowded a lot of living into a few brief years. He looked to be a man who could be a good friend or a ruthless enemy. Whistling a toneless tune a hundred bedded herds had known, he swung to cross the trestle spanning Crowfoot Gulch.

Danger awaited him at trail's end, he knew, but that was miles away and he had no inkling of peril as he forced his mount onto the tracks at the end of the trestle. His mount snorted and pawed, skittish of that spidery framework of timber and steel. The man spoke soothingly to the spooked horse. His patience saved his life.

In the center of the trestle a blue flame lashed upward like a devil's forking tongue and the silence of the night was wrenched asunder by a terrific blast, echoing and reechoing along the gulch. Dynamite! A giant's hand slapped horse and rider backward bodily just as the trestle bulged at its middle, then caved drunkenly in the boiling smoke.

Timbers rained from the sky and the Texan came out of his saddle on the fringe of that deadly downpour, his first astonishment at finding himself alive changing to a tremendous anger. This outrage was aimed at the Montana-Pacific, of course, but that didn't change the fact that it had almost claimed *his* life. No man could blast him off his horse!

Jerking a gun from beneath his slicker, he ran to the lip of the gulch. Smoke and dust stung his eyes as he peered downward, but faint moonlight filtered through the murky veil. Just below him, about ten feet down, on a ledge, a man hunkered, his back to the Texan.

The man's presence was proof enough that he'd had a hand in the dynamiting, and the Texan leaped, landing almost on top of the man. Instantly the fellow jerked around, wrapping brawny arms about the Texan. Then the two of them, locked in deadly embrace, were rolling and struggling on the narrow shelf.

There was no chance for the Texan to use his gun, but his adversary couldn't reach a weapon either. As they waged their silent, deadly fight, the Texan glimpsed his antagonist's face—a round face, seamed and leathery, with a rim of gray hair showing beneath the jammed-tight sombrero. He was an oldster, but he was stocky of body and mighty of arm. The Texan, in his mid-twenties, had the advantage of youth but his adversary was all whang-leather, and fighting with a desperation that made them equals in those first few moments.

Wriggling eel-like from the Texan's grasp, the older man lunged to his feet, tripping over his own spurs. He tottered on the edge of the ledge, clawing at the air, then vanished from view. The Texan pulled himself forward to see the man bounding and rolling downward into the gulch.

The slope was gradual and the oldster was going to stop up against a bush below, none the worse for his experience if luck favored him. There might be a second round of this fight and the Texan, anger still burning, ached to close with the man again. He would have followed him but at that instant he was jerked erect by a distant sound, the mournful wail of a locomotive.

A train was coming! Racing straight for the dynamited trestle! Had the engineer heard the sound of the explosion and guessed what lay ahead? Chances were he hadn't. Frantically the Texan clawed up the slope, starting a miniature avalanche of rocks and dirt until he finally stood panting and disheveled on the rim of the gulch. Then he was sprinting desperately down the track to stop that train.

His horse had bolted and he found it a quarter-mile from the trestle, stamping nervously. He was into the saddle at once, using spurs and the quirt that had been dangling from the saddle-horn. Already the rails were humming and the locomotive's headlight penciled a glare on a distant bluff. The Texan peeled off his slicker. Waving it wildly as he spurred forward, he prayed that the engineer would be alert.

Straight toward the Texan a bell-stacked engine roared and it took all of the rider's skill to hold his horse on the track, both blinded by the headlights' glow. He heard the squeal of brakes just as he jumped his horse off the track. Then the train—a dozen flatcars of steel with one passenger coach and a pusher engine behind—slid to a noisy stop.

The conductor was on the ground instantly and the engineer deserted his cab. But it was to a tall, soldierly-looking man who swiftly alighted from the passenger coach that the Texan turned. The look of a leader had marked Tyler Whitman for what he was.

"Trestle out—over the gulch!" the Texan panted. "Dynamited!"

"You're sure?" Whitman barked. "Who did it?"

"Couldn't say," the Texan confessed. "I tangled with one of 'em, but he got away. That bridge is shore busted."

A dozen men had crowded down the coach steps and Whitman spun upon them.

"Trestle's out!" he snapped. "You, Hanson! There's an emergency telegraph lay-out in the tool shack back a piece. Notify division headquarters. Tell 'em I want a cleanup crew here by sunup. Hammersmith! Arm six men and have a look around the gulch. While you're there, make an inventory of just exactly what we'll need."

There were other orders and the lieutenants of the railroad builder dispersed in a dozen different directions, each with an assignment. There was something of awe and admiration in the Texan's eyes as they followed Whitman.

Someone touched him and he turned to confront a girl who had come from the coach. She had dark hair, framing a face pretty enough to take the Texan's breath away. He was a six-footer, and she came just to his chin, he noticed. Her eyes were blue, he guessed, and big—but not with fear.

"I'm Lana Herndon," she said, and held out her hand. "I want to thank you. You saved the life of every one of us."

He took her hand, small and firm. "I just happened along," he muttered. "It might have been anybody."

He would have liked to say more, but Tyler Whitman unwittingly broke the spell by appearing suddenly, his hand outstretched.

"And now I've time to thank you properly," the railroad builder said. "For myself—and for the Montana-Pacific. I am Tyler Whitman, head of the road, and I owe you a great deal, sir. If there is anything I can ever do—"

The Texan pawed for the makings. "I could use a job," he said.

Tyler Whitman sized him up and because he had been of this whang-leather breed himself, he smiled.

"What can you do?"

"On a railroad? Reckon a branding iron would grow rusty, and you can't take the kinks out of a cast-iron cayuse. That leaves my fists and my gun."

"A trouble-shooter? I could use a dozen of them. It's a tough chore, man. There's Central Western trying to beat us and other forces buck us as well. Sabotage—agitators in our construction gangs, beef for the graders never arriving, leeches debauching our work crews. Do you want any part of our kind of work?"

"You've just hired yourself a man," said the Texan.

"You've got a horse and you can get to Caprock," said Whitman. "Dan Callishaw, my troubleshooter, is there. Report to him. Tell him I've hired you. He'll give you work to do." He spoke to a man at his elbow with something to report, then swung back. "Your name?" he asked the Texan.

"Name?" said the cowboy. "A man picks up a heap of names on a heap of trails. I packed a Bible up from Texas. I used it in a trail town where there was no preacher to say any words over a dead girl. They called me the Gospel Kid from then on. But if you've got to have something official for the records—put me down as Matt McGrath."

"McGrath!" Whitman echoed, his eyes widening.

"I savvy! Hank's kid brother! Now I know why there was something familiar about the lean look of you!"

"The Gospel Kid" grinned. "I got the Bible you sent me, Mr. Whitman, but it was a long time coming. Me, I never had the same address long. Likewise I got your letter. It said Hank had declared a one-man war on three skunks and was shot down."

"I thought you'd want the Bible," Whitman said. "Hank had a Texas address penciled beneath your name on the family record page. I took a chance on that." His eyes narrowed. "You're looking for the men who got Hank! You were joking about working for me!"

Ice glinted in the Kid's eyes.

"I crave to look along my gunsights at three gents," he said. "Them three are buckin' the Montana-Pacific, and I work for the road. But there's more to it than that. Hank craved to see a railroad in this country. It was his dream—but he didn't live to see it come true. I'd sorta like to have a hand in building a railroad for Hank." His voice softened and the ice went from his eyes. "You knew him, Mr. Whitman, but you never knew me. No two men born of the same woman was ever so different as me and Hank. He chose his trail, I chose mine. But he was my brother. See you in Caprock, boss."

He would have turned away then but he felt the tug of Lana Hendon's glance. The look she gave him was stony, and disgust was in it. It troubled the Kid, that look, for it was entirely opposite to her attitude before he had identified himself. Oh, well, he was working for the railroad now and he had his orders. Shrugging, he stepped up into saddle.

• Chapter 3 •

In Caprock the next day, the Gospel Kid found a town such as Hellvation Hank had never known. The railroad had come to Caprock and the streets were thronged—graders and gamblers and gunmen, steel layers and mule skinners, bridge builders and beef barons, and men whose calling was shady and nameless.

Once this town had known nothing more raucous than the revelry of a ranch crew celebrating pay-day, the bawling of a corraled beef herd awaiting a buyer's inspection. Now a medley of alien sounds made discord. Spring rains had turned the street into a muddy mire and along it moved ponderous freight wagons, the teamsters heaping blistering invective upon the toiling horses. Engines puffed and screamed at the sidings. Hammers and saws pounded and rasped while the drum of boots along the boardwalks was incessant. Caprock had blossomed into a sordid kind of splendor.

The Kid regarded it all, his sombrero thumbed back to reveal a shock of corn-colored hair, his thumbs hooked in his gunbelt. He was fascinated and disgusted at the same time. Yet it wasn't because of a religious leaning. He carried Hellvation Hank's bloodstained Bible in his shirtfront but his own trail had been smoky, and his ways violent.

Shrugging, he headed for the new pine-boarded building that was the railroad's office. A squat red-faced, redheaded Irishman who sat hunched over a telegraph instrument gave him the information he wanted.

"Dan Callishaw?" the telegrapher repeated. "Sure and it's up at the Drovers Rest ye'll be finding him. And yez can tell him Key O'Dade says there's a telegram here for him."

"I'm his new assistant," the Kid said. "I'll take it to him."

Key O'Dade regarded him from beneath a green eyeshade. "Then here it is, me bucko," he agreed. "Seeing as it's from Whitman, confirming the hiring of ye, I guess ye're the man to be delivering it."

At the Drovers Rest, after a word with the desk clerk, the Kid climbed the shabbily-carpeted stairway to drum his knuckles upon a door.

"Come in," called a voice. He stepped inside to confront a leveled gun.

In this room with its pine bureau, the inevitable pitcher and bowl, and iron bedstead, the man with the gun was the predominating figure—a short stubby fellow of indefinite age with a bulldog jaw and the flaring nostrils of a fighting man.

"Who are you?" he asked testily. "And what's your business?"

"Reckon this wire will explain," said the Kid.

Dan Callishaw laboriously read the telegram and pouched his gun. He grinned wryly as he extended his hand.

"Plumb sorry," he said. "A man has to be on the prod to keep on living in Caprock. But if Ty Whitman sent you, you're on the right side of the fence. McGrath, is it? No kin to Hellvation Hank?"

"Brother," said the Kid. "You knew him?"

Callishaw shook his head. "Heard a heap about him, though. I wasn't sent here until after Hank died. Whitman and Kurt Ormond, his chief engineer, were around here at the time, lining up things. Have a drink?"

The Kid's eyes, growing more accustomed to the semi-gloom, widened with astonishment as he saw what was standing in the corner nearest to the bed. A headboard for a grave—a new headboard made of pine! A precious commodity in this prairie country.

The painted lettering read:

HERE LIES DANIEL CALLISHAW
Born October 2, 18—
Died April 18, 18—
HE WAS WARNED, BUT HE
WOULDN'T LISTEN

Callishaw saw the Kid's surprise.

"Now," said the troubleshooter, "do you see why I unleather my gun before I open the door?"

"What's the idea?" said the Kid. "April eighteenth! Why, that's today!"

"A warning from The Three," Callishaw explained. "For me to get out by today. I found it in this room a couple weeks ago."

"The Three?"

"It's a name we've got for the bunch that's causing the Montana-Pacific all its grief. Ty Whitman started calling them The Three after Hellvation Hank spoke of three snakes. I find that pretty thing right handy for scratching matches when I hanker to smoke in bed."

But the Kid wasn't fooled. The man was worried—plenty worried. The Kid eyed the headboard again and a quick suspicion narrowed his eyes.

"But that first date?" he observed. "How could they know the date of your birth?"

"Thackery Weaver, the gent who runs the Caprock newspaper, gave me some publicity when I first hit town," Callishaw said. "See it?"

One stubby finger indicated a clipping pinned to the wall and the Kid ran his eyes over it. The heading read "AMONG US TODAY" and obviously was a regular feature of the newspaper. It began:

> Dan Callishaw, a representative of the Montana-Pacific Railroad who has lately been assigned to duty in Caprock, has had a colorful career. Callishaw first saw the light of day in Indiana where he was born on October 2nd, 18—. . . .

There was a lurid description of the subsequent doings of Dan Callishaw, troubleshooter. The Kid's curiosity was satisfied. Anybody in Caprock might have prepared the weird wooden warning.

"You think they'll try for you today?" the Kid asked.

Callishaw shrugged. "Maybe. Probably bluff, though. It's one thing to name the day of a man's death. It's another to make sure he dies on that day. But it sure gives a man something to think about."

The Kid had to agree. He dismissed the matter, eyeing his superior woodenly.

"Where do I start to work?" he asked.

"Work?" said Callishaw. "There'll be work for twenty like us, from now on. It's been a bad winter and M.P. just barely got beyond Caprock. But a new season's opening and we'll be heading for Lazura fast. Then's when hell will start to pop. The dynamite job that Ty mentions in his telegram is just an eye opener. We could use a troop of soldiers but the Government can't see our need for them, even if a batch of bluecoats are hunkering on their haunches down at Fort

Yellowstone. The Union Pacific had soldier protection. That was because the Indians were lifting hair in them days. We're fighting an outfit just as crafty and just as tough!''

He paused, arching one eyebrow. ''You eat yet?'' he asked abruptly, and the Kid shook his head. ''Go get some grub under your belt, McGrath,'' Callishaw went on. ''Then we'll head for the grading camp. Kurt Ormond's at end o' steel complainin' that the crews are dissatisfied and sullen. We'll see if we can stomp the snake that's keeping 'em that way.''

That suited the Kid, for inactivity weighed heavily upon him. In a nearby restaurant, a gloomy place smelling of grease and dirt, he found a table for himself. The place was filled and waitresses were hurrying everywhere. While the Kid waited, he took the Bible from his shirtfront and fished into his pockets for a pencil stub and a scrap of paper. The Bible was at his elbow but he didn't refer to it as he scribbled three verses absently:

> And there went out a champion of the camp of the Philistines, Goliath of Gath whose height was six cubits and a span.
>
> When Herod the king had heard these things, he was troubled, and all Jerusalem with him.
>
> Then one of the twelve called Judas Iscariot when unto the chief priests . . . to betray him.

The Kid frowned at the words he had written, and even after food was placed before him, his mind was still upon the riddle of those three references.

The letter Whitman had written when he'd sent Hellvation Hank's Bible to Matt McGrath had not been too informative. Hank had threatened to expose three men. Hank had been killed. That was the size of it.

Three men. . . .

At first Matt McGrath had seen no significance in those three bloodstained passages in his brother's Bible. Then he'd begun to read a meaning in them, for those three passages referred to three Biblical characters. Matt McGrath knew little about the Book but he'd taken to studying it after that, and slowly he had begun to understand why those passages had been marked. And that was when he had packed his warbag and taken the long trail north—in search of three men.

Goliath was one of them, a man of great strength. But Samson had been a strong man, too. Why hadn't Hellvation Hank marked a reference to Samson instead of Goliath? Now the Kid thought he saw the answer. Samson had used his strength for good—Goliath had championed evil. And there was a clue.

Herod? The king of Judea had been a puzzler for the Kid and he had searched long and diligently for the key to the character of that man, dead almost two thousand years. Herod, crafty and cruel and unscrupulous, an evil king, jealous of his sovereignty, a red-handed man who'd had lesser men do his killing for him.

And Judas, the betrayer. There was the simplest of the three to decode.

There was one other significance, the Kid decided. Obviously the three men did not have Biblical given names. No Pete or Jake or Joe had struck down Hellvation Hank. If such had been the case, the sky pilot would have marked a reference to Peter, Jacob or Joseph.

His hunger satisfied, the Kid came to the street again. If there was a man in Caprock who might know the enemies of the Montana-Pacific who had traits resembling those of Goliath, Herod and Judas, that man was Dan Callishaw whose job was to battle "The Three." He'd ask Callishaw about them.

A thousand sounds beat against him as he skipped nimbly across the muddy street.

Two freighters, their wagons wheel-locked hub against hub, cursed each other roundly, and on a nearby corner a drunken man, his shirttail out and flapping, lifted a gun and fired into the sky, punctuating the shots with a declaration that he was a curly wolf and therefore entitled to howl. And on this street where sin strode boldly, that roaring gun attracted no attention.

Truly, the Kid observed to himself, with a wry grin, this town was feeling its oats. The thought kept him company up the gloomy stairway and to Dan Callishaw's door. He tapped on the door.

"It's me, McGrath, Dan!" he called in a loud voice, and stepped into the darkened room.

Dan Callishaw was here but now he was a shapeless sprawling thing, heaped in a corner, and there was no life in him, for a bullet had torn off the top of his head. In falling he had somehow crashed against the headboard tilted against the wall and his body pinned it there, half concealing it. All the Kid could read was that last line:

HE WAS WARNED, BUT HE
WOULDN'T LISTEN.

• CHAPTER 4 •

MANY BUSINESSES HAD BOOMED IN CAPROCK WITH the coming of the steel, but Hoyt Durham's Golden Slipper Saloon had reaped the greatest share of the golden harvest. Trade had been many times multiplied by the influx of railroad workers who sought the solace of the bottle, the green baize, or the painted smiles of percentage girls.

A long bar ran the length of the Golden Slipper. There was a spacious floor for dancing while a gambling wing hummed to the click of the roulette wheels, the incessant slap of the pasteboards. Oil paintings adorned the walls. Most of them depicted semi-nudes and one in particular held the place of honor, a huge painting called "The Lady of the Nile" which portrayed a voluptuous, sultry-eyed woman stretched full length upon a leopard skin, a diaphanous bit of cloth flowing about her.

On the second floor were the rooms of the percentage girls, and another room which no more than a dozen men had ever entered. It was Hoyt Durham's private office, luxuriously furnished as befitted the man who ruled the shadowy side of the range.

Three men sat in that room on the morning of Matt McGrath's arrival in Caprock. One was Hoyt Durham, dark-skinned and dandified, thin-faced and with a wisp of mustache and a nervous habit of preening it with one jewel-bedecked hand. Another man was Curly Bottsinger, the broad-shouldered freight line owner, a huge hulking giant, shaggy and powerful as a rampaging grizzly.

A lamp lighted the room, even in the daytime, for there were no windows, since the office was below the floor level of the second story. The third man sat in the shadows, just beyond the fringe of the yellow light. He was studying the two, and his thought was that Hoyt Durham was the deadlier of the pair in spite of the primitive savagery of Bottsinger.

"I had to wait," Bottsinger was saying. "This other gent was in the room with Callishaw for quite a spell. I tried to listen to what they was jawin' about. As much as I could get was that this jigger had been sent to side Callishaw—another troubleshooter. I hid in the hall till the new jigger left."

"Yes?" the third man prompted him.

"I knocked and Callishaw let me in. He had that old Peacemaker of his in his fist and he wasn't in no hurry about pouchin' it. 'I just come in from end o' steel," I said to him. "I got news for you, Dan.' He relaxed some then, puttin' his gun away. Then I let him have it and got out in a hurry."

"Positive he was dead?" the third man asked.

"Plumb dead," Bottsinger insisted.

"Anybody notice the shot?"

"Reckon not. Some drunk was blazin' at the sky down on the corner and there was a cap or two bein' cracked out in the alley. What difference did another shot make?"

The third man settled back in his chair contentedly.

"Business is good, eh Hoyt?" he observed. "Gentlemen, you're a pair of scoundrels. You, Hoyt, are bucking the Montana-Pacific and all the while lining your pockets with railroad payroll money. And you, Curly—you're getting fat on grading contracts and the money you're paid to haul freight past the end of steel. Biting the hand that feeds you."

"So?" Hoyt Durham said, smiling without humor. "Business was good before the railroad came, especially if a man lifted a little beef in the dark of the moon as a sideline. But what happens when the road is finished? The boom is over and law and order comes to the Caprock country."

"Me, I hate every cussed tie they lay!" Bottsinger exploded savagely. "Look at the cinch thing I had! If a man wanted something hauled on or off this range, he paid my price and liked it. And if some jigger got the notion of starting a rival freight line, things happened to that gent. But now trains are running as far as Caprock already. I'll be bankrupt once this road goes through. I shore wish Tyler Whitman had been dumped into Crowfoot Gulch last night with that load of steel on top of him! It was only fool luck that saved him after me and the boys blasted that trestle."

The third man still smiled, the satisfied smile of a man whose allies are his pawns. Bottsinger folded one hairy fist and regarded it truculently. Durham stirred restlessly.

"What next?" the saloon owner asked. "Think we ought to send that new troubleshooter a headboard?"

"That headboard idea's no good!" Bottsinger scoffed. "It didn't make Callishaw run."

"The headboard idea," the third man explained patiently, "has a psychological value, Curly. You wouldn't understand that. Its value is twice as great because Callishaw wouldn't be warned and had to die. The next man to get one of those wooden warnings is going to know it means what it implies."

"We should send one to that new troubleshooter," Durham insisted. "We want to get rid of him pronto."

"Not yet," the third man decided. "The fellow will probably walk softly once he learns what happened to Callishaw, anyway. Our job right now is at end o' steel. Curly, you'd better get out there again. With winter really over Whitman's order will be to drive, and drive hard. Keep the men stirred up enough so they'll do about half their work. Tell 'em M.P. is going broke and they'll never be paid. Tell 'em Central Western is paying better money. Tell 'em anything. Every delay means the Montana-Pacific is that much nearer to being licked."

"And C.W. is that much nearer to crossing the Big Thunders first," Durham added. "That will please you, eh? And us too. Montana's big enough to have a railroad without it running through the Caprock country to spoil our business."

Curly Bottsinger came to his feet and moved in his ponderous fashion to the wall that separated this office from the barroom. A leather flap, about four inches square, hung on the wall about three feet above the floor. Crouching, Bottsinger lifted it to peer through two eye-holes bored in the wall. He was looking down into the barroom through the eyes of "The Lady of the Nile." The picture was a trick affair and an ingenious one. The eyes of the painting were not on the canvas but on the leather flap. When the flap hung in place, which it usually did, the picture looked complete to the keenest observer. When the flap was lifted, human eyes took the place of the painted ones.

Curly Bottsinger scanned the big room through the device. Gazing long and intently, he stiffened with excitement and straightened himself, his broad face twisted.

"It's him!" he said huskily. "He just walked in!"

"Who?" the third man demanded quickly.

"The new troubleshooter. The one who was confabbin' with Dan Callishaw this morning. But that ain't all! I had a pretty fair look at that jigger this morning. But just for a minute as he stood inside the batwings there was something about his face that—that . . . Hell, I would have swore he was Hellvation Hank McGrath!"

"Hellvation Hank," Hoyt Durham said emphatically, "is dead and buried!"

The anonymous man crossed the room in two strides and crouched to have a look for himself.

"He does look like McGrath," he agreed.

Curly Bottsinger was dragging a gun from its holster. "Hoyt, I'm going to plumb ruin your pretty pitcher," he snarled. "Maybe that jigger saw me around the Drovers Rest this morning. He's here lookin' for me! I'm going to drive a bullet right between the eyes of 'The Lady of the Nile' and likewise right between the eyes of that new troubleshooter!"

"Wait, you fool!" snapped the third man. His fingers closed on Bottsinger's wrist. "There's half-a-hundred railroad workers down there. If a man is gunned right before their eyes they'll come stampeding up here and tear the place apart. I know the breed! Even if we got out it wouldn't take Tyler whitman ten minutes to add up things, either. He'd know The Three he talks about are using the Golden Slipper for headquarters."

"But we can't let that jigger go snoopin' around here," Bottsinger argued.

The eyes of the third man were dark with thought. At last he smiled.

"I have it!" he said. "I'd thought we'd let this new fellow alone for a while unless opportunity laid him in our laps. Perhaps it has—if we work it right. I've got a plan that will do the trick. Listen, gentlemen—"

• Chapter 5 •

For a long time the Gospel Kid had stood in the musty room in the Drovers Rest, looking down at the body of Dan Callishaw. Then, knowing life was forever gone from the man, he went downstairs and told the clerk who promptly sped along the street to the undertaker's. The Kid headed for the railroad office to send a telegram.

"Can you get this through to Tyler Whitman?" he asked Key O'Dade, handing him his scribbled message.

O'Dade read it, a growing anger making his red face redder.

"Dan Callishaw—dead!" he gasped. "So it's killin' good men they've taken to doin'! Bad cess to the three of them. Bad cess!"

"O'Dade," said the Kid, "if you wanted to find the gun that shot Dan Callishaw, where would you start lookin'?"

Key O'Dade gave him a quick glance, running his stubby finger through his red hair.

"Faith and it's a riddle yez are askin' me, boy. But it's the Golden Slipper where ye'll find gunmen hanging out and it's Hoyt Durham that's hirin' thim these days. Just this mornin' two new ones was askin' the way to that divil's own dancehall."

"The Golden Slipper, eh?" said the Kid and turned on his heel.

Looking for the killer of Dan Callishaw in this teeming town would be like looking for a needle in a haystack—or worse, since he had no idea who'd triggered the gun. But there was always the chance that luck might favor a man, some odd clue might come his way. That possibility took the Kid through the batwings and into the glittering interior of the Golden Slipper.

Fifty-odd M.P. workers awaited the hour when the work train would pull out for end o' steel. Most of them were in this saloon, crowding the bar or milling in the gambling wing. There were others here as well, gamblers and gunmen, and the Kid, standing in the doorway, had the sensation of eyes upon him. Something prickled along his spine, some vague warning. Yet his darting glance saw no hostility. He moved to the bar, ordered whisky.

A great mirror, freighted in a decade before, ran the length of the wall behind the bar and in the polished glass he studied the place and the people who filled it. The paintings on the wall claimed his attention, too, for he could see their reflections.

But it was the one called "The Lady of the Nile" that really claimed his eyes. Just for an instant that picture had come to life! It was unbelievable, but in was so! For a second there had been a subtle change in the lifeless canvas, a change the Kid was unable to define. His eyes glued to the picture, he watched it intently, hoping the change would come again. He was still watching when a voice spoke at his elbow.

"Pretty, ain't she?"

The man who had edged up to the bar beside him

was a seedy specimen, gaunt, cadaverous, with bleary eyes in a face that hadn't felt a razor in at least three days. Thin yellow hair, ragged and unkempt, fell to the collar of the corduroy coat the man wore. The suit had obviously been slept in. The brand of a barfly was so plainly stamped on the fellow that the Kid anticipated his next remark.

"I'm down on my luck," the man whined. "Could you buy a feller a drink?"

The Kid eyed him reflectively. "Been around here long?" he asked.

"Months now. Ever since last fall."

The Kid signaled a bartender and ordered a bottle and a second glass. Wincing at the boomtown price he was forced to pay, he wondered if the investment would bring any worthwhile returns. His guest slopped liquor into the glass, downed it in a gulp. The Kid sipped his.

"Who," he asked, faint irony in his voice, "do I have the pleasure of drinking with?"

"Loomis. Shadow Loomis they call me. What difference does a name make?"

The Kid had no answer for that one. But he automatically responded to the demands of courtesy.

"McGrath is my name," he volunteered.

"I know," said Loomis. "He was killed." "Shadow" Loomis poured himself another drink without waiting for an invitation. "He shouldn't have opened the door without a gun," he said morosely. "He shouldn't have taken that chance."

The Kid felt a swift surge of excitement, but his voice betrayed none of it.

"What do you know about that?" he asked easily. "How do you know he opened the door without a gun?"

Shadow Loomis shrugged. "How does anybody know? He was found dead in front of his own shack and there was no gun on him . . . A pretty picture there on the wall, eh? 'The Lady of the Nile' they call her. She can see, friend, and she can hear. And some day she'll speak. Just remember that Shadow Loomis told you."

The Kid looked at Loomis in disgust as the barfly poured another drink. The man was crazy, the Kid decided, or at least so addle-witted from too much alcohol as to be hardly worth bothering with, for his mouthings were certainly meaningless. But as the Kid shifted his gaze to the mirror, studying the man in its polished depths, his own eyes narrowed thoughtfully.

"You kin to Hellvation Hank?" Loomis asked, dragging a sleeve across his mouth.

Before the Kid could answer, that presentiment of danger ran through him again. But the warning bell tolled too late, for suddenly danger was an actuality rather than a shadowy foreboding. It happened fast.

A man had crowded to the bar beside the Kid, a tall, angular man, beard-stubbled and loose-lipped.

"Give a feller elbow room, can't you!" the man growled, and shouldered the Kid away so violently as to send him staggering backward to crash against another man.

This other fellow, barrellike in build, cursed him viciously. "Watch where yuh're goin'!" he snarled and shoved the Kid, hurling him back against the first man.

The play was so well timed, so patently a planned job of troublemaking that it shrieked a warning to the Kid. The anger that blazed in the eyes of both these men was completely out of proportion to what prompted it, while the tied down holsters of the two proclaimed their calling—and their intent. Others saw the play and read its portent. Suddenly men were falling over each other in a mad scramble to get out of the possible line of fire.

Shadow Loomis had slid away as silently as though he were made of the substance of his sobriquet. The Kid stood alone with the two men, one on either side of him. He was at an angle where they would catch him in a raking crossfire once they went for their guns. And that was what they were going to do, just as soon as they found a halfway plausible excuse.

"Get at it!" the Kid said with a vast disgust.

They needed no further invitation. The Kid, facing the taller of the two, didn't need to see the man's downward darting hand, for the gesture registered in the fellow's yellowish eyes. Instantly the Kid was twisting aside, jerking his own gun in the same motion. The walls sent back hammering echoes as two guns roared. The Kid fell sideward to the floor. The tall gunman fell too, drilled through the heart.

But only one dead man sprawled upon the floor. The gunman's bullet had breathed hotly past the Kid's ear, missing him. He had purposely fallen to save himself from the other gunman and the ruse had worked, for a bullet had droned over his head as he fell. Hitting the floor, the Kid rolled, the next shot from the squat gunman geysering dust into his eyes. But firing from the floor, the Kid saw the man take three hesitant steps, then trip over his partner to fall dead on top of him.

The Kid came to his feet, gun still in his hand, his eyes flickering from one face to another, measuring the men who crowded against the far wall.

"Which one of you is Hoyt Durham?" he demanded in the hush that held the crowd.

From the shelter of a post supporting the ceiling, Hoyt Durham stepped, his swarthy face as expressionless as the top of a table.

"I'm Durham, stranger," he said. "Some mighty nice shooting you did. What can I do for you?"

"These your men?"

Durham stroked his mustache, his gaze sliding over the two dead gunmen.

"They came here this morning asking for a job," he said. "A man in my position has to have others to guard his back sometimes, but I have no use for men of their stripe. I turned them down. That's what put them on the prod, probably."

Stooping, the Kid turned one of the dead gunmen's pockets inside out. A handful of gold coins tinkled to the floor. The Kid scattered them with the toe of his boot as he straightened.

"Probably!" he said mockingly.

His gaze locked with Hoyt Durham's and in that instant a name drummed through the Kid's head persistently. *Herod!* A red-handed king who had lesser men do his killing for him. But because there wasn't a shred of proof to back his suspicions, he pouched his gun and strode out without another word.

As he shouldered along the crowded walk, a reckless anger was burning within him. He found himself abreast of a building whose big bay window bore the lettering:

CAPROCK TRIBUNE
Thackery Weaver, Editor

He turned inside. Enthroned behind a huge pigeonholed desk in a littered room redolent of ink and glue, sat a plump, pink-cheeked, gray-headed man who blinked owlishly through a pair of thick glasses.

"You Weaver?" the Kid asked.

"That's me," the man admitted. "Can I help you?"

"You can answer a question," said the Kid. "You gave Dan Callishaw a write-up in your paper, a write-up that mentioned everything about him, includin' the date of his birth. Do you always make it a point to find out a man's birthday?"

Thackery Weaver beamed pridefully. "The Caprock *Tribune* boasts of its thoroughness," he said. "We find it pays to be alert. In our files we have complete lists of data on anybody of importance. Should a piece of news break, we can instantly embellish it with all the necessary details."

"I savvy," the Kid said. "You could practically write an obituary ahead of time. You've got a finger on everybody in town, eh?"

"Anybody who is prominent. I can supply the date of birth, the place, the past history of all our leading citizens including newcomers like Tyler Whitman and Kurt Ormond, his chief engineer."

"I'd like a look at those lists," the Kid interjected.

Thackery Weaver came out of his chair. He was short and pudgy, and if he hoped to look belligerent he only looked ludicrous.

"Just who are you, mister?" he demanded in a less cordial tone.

"Troubleshooter for the M.P.," the Kid said. "Trot out those lists. I crave to see just who's included."

Weaver hesitated, shrugged, and moved over to an old-fashioned filing cabinet that stood against one ink-smudged wall. Dragging out a drawer, he fumbled in its depths for several minutes. When he turned, his pink jowls sagged with amazement.

"They're gone!" he cried. "My lists are gone—stolen! What do you know about this, mister? What made you so interested in them?"

"Never mind," said the Kid.

He was studying the little newspaper man, trying to read Thackery Weaver's character and to fit it into one of the three patterns. But Weaver was hard to read. Those glasses made him so for they distorted his appearance.

"What do you think about the railroad?" the Kid asked casually. "Any reason why it shouldn't run through this section?"

"The railroad?" Weaver repeated, and instantly struck a pose. "The railroad is the dream of every far-sighted citizen of Caprock and our paper was the first to point out the benefits to come from such an undertaking. Why, in an early editorial of mine—"

"That's enough," the Kid said brusquely, then softened his tone. "I'm thankin' you for your trouble. And here's a tip for you. There's news for your paper at the Drovers Rest and the Golden Slipper today. Better go after it."

Weaver reached quickly for paper and pencil.

"News!" he cried excitedly. "But you're news too. I'd like to give you a write-up. Now if you'll just give me some data—"

"No, thanks," the Kid said drily, and left.

At the railroad office he found a characteristically brief telegram for him from Whitman. It read:

SORRY ABOUT CALLISHAW, YOU'RE PROMOTED. REPORT TO ORMOND.

The work train was chugging out of Caprock and the Kid made it on the run. He found a seat in a car overcrowded with graders and steel layers and, hunkered there, he recalled something he had completely forgotten in the excitement of the gun duel. Shadow Loomis . . . That man might be a piece to the puzzle too. Apparently Loomis was a dissolute barfly, yet he didn't play the part to perfection. Watching him in the mirror, the Kid had seen Loomis step out of character, but hadn't had a chance to do anything about the discovery.

Shadow Loomis had begged for liquor and downed his first drink. The Kid wasn't so sure about the others. But one thing was certain—Shadow Loomis had poured his last drink into the cuspidor at his feet.

• CHAPTER 6 •

END O' STEEL!

The Gospel Kid reached it in the late afternoon and with his neck craned from a window of the work train he had his first glimpse of the scene. Beyond Caprock the jerky march of the rails to the mountains had been halted by the icy hand of a Montana winter. But now the Montana-Pacific was stirring to activity like a hibernating bear freshly released from its season of bondage.

Weather-beaten tents and construction shacks mottled the prairie. Supplies were scattered everywhere. The bridge crews were a score of miles ahead and beyond them a tunnel crew was already drilling a hole through the first barrier of the Big Thunders. But most of the workers were here, a teeming army of them.

Standing on a siding was a special car with a lonely sort of dignity—the office of the engineering staff. The Kid crossed to it. In the car he found Kurt Ormond busy at a desk piled high with reports and papers.

Waiting for Ormond to be free, the Kid studied the man who was second in command to Tyler Whitman. He was surprised to see that Ormond was apparently little older than thirty; a still-faced, sharp-featured man, browned by exposure. The Kid wasn't sure whether he liked Ormond or not. The chief engineer had a machinelike quality that made him as impersonal as a donkey engine. When Ormond spoke, that was emphasized in his metallic voice.

"Well?"

"Whitman told me to report to you," the Kid explained. "I'm McGrath, the new troubleshooter. Dan Callishaw is dead."

"I know," Ormond said. "I just got a wire from O'Dade. If Whitman hired you, that settles it. But I'm not so sure it was a good idea."

"You don't like my looks, eh?"

"I've nothing personal against you," Ormond said. "I just happen to know a lot about you. Ty knows those same things and hired you, anyway. Your brother, Hellvation Hank, was a man in anybody's language, but you're a different kind of gent. You were mixed up in a few shady deals down in Texas, McGrath, and we know it. Your backtrail makes no difference to me, so long as you play square with the Montana-Pacific. But I'm wondering. When the road is fighting for its life, I'm not so sure I want a man around whose history has as many missing pages as yours. Do we understand each other?"

"I reckon," the Kid said, without rancor. "Anything else?"

"You're here to avenge your brother," Ormond went on. "I can read that in your eyes. It would please M.P. mightily if you caught up with The Three, but the railroad comes first, if you're working for us. Maybe you'll be off riding your own trail just when we most need you."

"Me, I've got two jobs to do," said the Kid. "One

of them is to see M.P. steel cross the Big Thunders. That would be for Hank—but maybe you wouldn't understand that. If I have to do my other chore first, I'll quit the railroad. Right now I crave to go to work. Callishaw said something about an agitator being here. Maybe I should have a look-see around."

Ormond nodded. "Somebody's stirring up the crews," he admitted. "I haven't had the time to try and smoke him out. Some of the work is let out on contract, which means a lot of strange faces around camp. Go have a look—but be careful."

The Kid paused at the door. "Met a queer gent in Caprock today," he said. "Shadow Loomis he calls himself. Know him?"

Ormond's interest quickened. "Yes," he said. "Looks like a barfly but I've wondered about him. If you get a chance, McGrath, have a long talk with him and see just what you can find out."

The Kid stepped from the car. Kurt Ormond had been blunt, outspoken, but the Kid carried no grudge on that score. They each had a job to do. Part of Ormond's job had been to weigh Matt McGrath for any weakness he might find. That was as it should be.

Blending with the toiling crews, the Kid made an unobtrusive tour of inspection, seeing men who worked hard and men who worked lazily and studying all of them in silence. There was a certain advantage in the fact that he was new here. His presence didn't spur the lazy to a pretense of industry. The Kid wasn't concerned with lazy men—it was something sinister he sought. And within an hour he found it.

Far out on the grade, when a score of men leveled the roadbed, their pace determined the pace of those who came behind them—the track layers and those husky men who swung the sledges to inch the rails toward the west. Here was the key to the trouble that slowed down work. The Kid saw them loitering, saw them put their heads together for whispered consultations time and again while those behind had to wait.

The straw boss of this sluggish crew was a broad-shouldered giant who had been on the work train out. The Kid sized up the man purposefully and finally tapped his shoulder.

"I'd like to talk to you," he said.

The giant turned and for an instant he stood slack-jawed, his eyes widening. Then his lip curled as he surveyed the Kid from head to foot.

"Texas man, eh?" he said. "I saw you in the Golden Slipper today. You're mighty handy with your gun but I never knew a Tejano yet that was worth two cents without his hardware. I got nothing to talk to you about. Get out o' here, mister, before you get trampled on!"

Kurt Ormond was striding toward them and the Kid waited for the chief engineer's arrival.

"Stick around, Ormond," he said. "I've found the gent we was talking about, I'm thinkin'."

"You're crazy!" Ormond snapped while the Kid slipped off his gun-belt. "It's Curly Bottsinger you're bucking. He's the toughest rough-and-tumble man in the Caprocks. Do you want to get killed?"

"Shucks," said the Kid. "The Caprocks ain't so big. You gents ever seen the Panhandle?"

He hit Bottsinger then. His left fist arched to smash bunched knuckles into the giant's face, a terrific blow. It was the quickest way to get things started, the Kid had decided, for he knew he had found the man who was delaying the steel. That man was the kind who could understand no argument but action.

But the blow scarcely shook Bottsinger. He came forward with a wild rush and the Kid was cold with the realization that it had been a great deal easier to start this fight then it was going to be to finish it.

Bottsinger's fists lashed out as the Kid bobbed beneath them. For a single second the giant was off balance and in that golden moment the Kid's right whammed against Bottsinger's chin. The giant only laughed, his own fist swinging. The Kid saw it coming—saw it too late. He tried to twist aside but Bottsinger's knuckles grazed his shoulder, sending the Kid somersaulting backwards onto the ground.

With a roar of triumph Bottsinger came after him and the giant's intent was obvious. It was going to be a rough-and-tumble fight now, the kind of fight where the immense bulk of Bottsinger would be an overwhelming advantage. But as the giant launched himself upon the fallen Texan, the Kid rolled to his back and his legs jackknifed, his boots crashing against Bottsinger's broad chest, hurling the man away. Before Bottsinger could recover himself to rush again, the Kid was on his feet and carrying the fight to him, his arms pistoning.

They crashed together, slugging toe to toe until the Kid turned himself into a dancing, darting figure, hard to find and harder to hit. All the while his own fists were taking toll of the giant and cheers went up, for an unofficial recess had suddenly been declared and every worker ringed the fighters, yelling, excited, shouting advice that was only a dull roar in the ears of the Kid.

It was a battle that was to go down in the annals of the Montana-Pacific and at first the Kid was sick with the thought that its end was inevitable. He had tackled Bottsinger because it was part of his job, but there was another reason as well. Kurt Ormond had been dubious about the Kid—and not entirely without justification. Here was the chance to prove himself. Then he'd wondered if he had bitten off a great deal more than he was going to be able to chew.

But he was still on his feet, still slugging, and it came to him that he had worn the fine edge from the fighting strength of Curly Bottsinger. The man was still before him, a red, blurry shadow that refused to go down. But Bottsinger's blows had less dynamite behind them. The Kid threw himself into the fray with a fresh fervor, born of a faint glimmer of hope.

He ripped rights and lefts at Bottsinger's body and face, taking punishment while dodging the giant's malletlike fists with an automatic efficiency. Once when they went down together, Bottsinger's thumb fumbled for the Kid's eye. But the Kid managed to heave him aside, come erect again, and the giant came after him.

Then it was an endless repetition of what had become a nightmare—slug and dodge, hit and ride with a blow, drive and drive and drive until that bloody bulk was before him no more.

He was like a man in a troubled dream whose motions are sluggish when speed is needed, whose strength is water when it had to be steel. He feinted awkwardly, his gesture threatening Bottsinger's midriff. The giant dropped his huge fists for protection and his jaw was exposed. The Kid had hit that jaw a dozen times but he hit it again, hit it with everything that was left. Bottsinger fell, sprawling loosely on the ground.

But he would be up again. He would be back with those merciless fists flailing, and the Kid would go down. He knew that. He could gauge his own powers and knew he had gone to their limit. But something was decidedly wrong, for Bottsinger wasn't getting up. Bottsinger was staying on the ground. Spitting out a tooth, Bottsinger forced a single word through his broken lips:

"Enough."

Bottsinger was beaten! And horny hands were seizing the Kid and a hundred men were surrounding him, pounding his back, trying to shake his hand. But there was strength enough in him to speak and he did, his voice sounding nothing like his own.

"Gents," he said, "I'm no great shakes with a shovel but I'd like to see this road finished. I reckon you'll have to do the rest of it. Back to it, you terriers!"

They were a fighting breed, and they could understand a fighting man. They returned to the grade enthusiastically and only the Kid, weak and dizzy, stood there with Kurt Ormond while Bottsinger painfully propped himself upon one elbow.

"You're a McGrath all right, curse you!" the giant snarled. "Hellvation Hank was the only man your size who ever packed your kind of wallop!"

"Get out when you're able!" the Kid said wearily. "Get out—and stay out!"

There was admiration in Ormond's eyes.

"You just manhandled the giant of the Caprock country!" the engineer said.

"A giant?" the Kid repeated, and shook his head. " 'And there went out a champion out of the camp of the Philistines,' " he muttered, " 'named Goliath of Gath . . .' "

"What's that?" Ormond asked.

The Kid made no answer for it was no more than a hunch he had. But there was balm for his bruised body in the thought that perhaps he had just met up with another of The Three, and beaten the man.

• Chapter 7 •

On his first day in the service of the Montana-Pacific, the Kid had had his baptism of fire and of fist, conquered a champion, and won the respect of the brawny breed who pushed steel toward the sunset. If the days that followed were not so hectic, they were busy, with the Kid policing the grading crews and stamping out the last of the dissension among them. There was excitement too, and danger, for another trestle was blasted skyward and there were nights when the Kid never saw the cot in the tent that had been assigned to him. But his was the satisfaction of having done his part when the end of steel reached Lazura in record time.

A mile a day, sometimes more as April turned into May, the track had crawled, and the first of June saw the railroad's arrival at Lazura. And Lazura took on a new lease of life for the bubble had burst at Caprock and the wise ones hurried to this new font of fortune. Even the Golden Slipper made the move. True, this was a new Golden Slipper, a flimsy building of wood and canvas designed for transportation from town to town. But the same bar and tables were here, freighted overland by Curly Bottsinger. And "The Lady of the Nile" smiled down from a fragile wall upon the thirsty of Lazura-town.

Thackery Weaver was here, too, his press pounding in a big tent. The Kid met the editor on the street and had to listen to Weaver's enthusiastic babbling.

"It's not the Caprock *Tribune* any more. It's the paper that follows the rails, the *End O'Steel Echo*. When the road is finished, I'll go back to Caprock." He fixed his weird stare upon the Kid, his voice peevish as another thought struck him. "Why didn't you tell me you were Hellvation Hank's brother? Everybody knows it now and everybody knows you're here to avenge Hank. I could have given you a mighty nice write-up. . . ."

The Kid shouldered on. A score of business places were hanging out shingles, all proving that Caprock was following the steel. In a dark alley that first night, the Kid caught a glimpse of a phantomlike figure scurrying along and was sure it was Shadow Loomis. He chased the man, calling his name, but Loomis merged with the gloom and was gone. Yet the Kid was certain he'd seen Shadow Loomis, and the puzzle remained.

A great restlessness was beginning to stir within Matt McGrath. The novelty of the grading camps had worn off, and the marching days had brought him no nearer to his goal. Of course he was seeing the triumph of the Montana-Pacific for word came that the Central Western's progress was not alarming. That pleased the Kid, since the railroad was Hellvation Hank's unrealized dream. But he was no nearer to The Three and he longed for a change in routine. So it was that Tyler Whitman found him more than responsive when he gave the Kid a special order.

"You'll find the Deadman country yonder," Whitman told him, a wave of his arm indicating the Big Thunders looming above them, miles away yet seemingly at the end of the steel. "There's a beef herd being gathered on that range for delivery to the camps. I'd rest easier if you'd meet the herd and make sure it got here."

"Rustlers?" the Kid asked hopefully.

"Maybe. Or perhaps the herd never was gathered."

"Don't the Deadman ranchers like the feel of railroad money?"

Whitman frowned. "You might as well know the truth of it," he said. "Storm Herndon of the H-in-a-Hat is king of the Deadman range and a crusty old codger he is. He hates the railroad and makes no bones about it, figures it will fill the country with sod-busters. Yet Herndon is a friend of mine. We rode range together, along with Hellvation Hank, before we had fuzz on our faces. But if Herndon's got it into his head to buck the road, he'll fight hard. If he decides to starve us out, the other Deadman ranchers will probably follow his lead. See what you might be up against?"

"Herndon?" said the Kid. "There was a girl on the train into Caprock, name of Lana Herndon."

"His daughter," Whitman explained. "Storm sent her East for schooling. She didn't like it, and she's just as stubborn as he is."

The Kid asked no more questions, but another hour found him in the saddle and out on the plain. Pushing hard that long day, he passed Deadman-town, sleepy and silent, awaiting the magic wand of the Montana-Pacific to awake it from its drowsiness, and he ate with the M.P. tunnel crew upon the slope of the Big Thunders that night. Dawn found him angling northward, skirting that frowning range.

It was wild, rugged country with upthrusting ground forming a palisade of cliffs with a stream gurgling at their base. These cliffs were an effective barrier forcing the M.P. to swing to the south. The engineering staff had decided to detour before drilling a tunnel. But such matters held little interest for the Kid. Circling back on the prairie again, he scanned the horizon and in the late afternoon saw the dust raised by a thousand hoofs as a moving queue of cattle moved stolidly across the range.

A half dozen riders hazed the beefs along. There was no chuckwagon with the outfit but an open-topped wagon, piled high with supplies, led the cavalcade in the point position, a small figure holding the reins. Touching spurs to his horse, the Kid thundered toward the wagon, whirling his mount to rein short abreast of it.

"Railroad beef?" he asked, and found himself staring into the blue eyes of Lana Herndon.

She was in levis and jumper with her hair tucked under a floppy sombrero. The Kid stared, tongue-tied. This girl had crowded his thoughts many times since their brief meeting beyond Crowfoot Gulch but mostly he had remembered the coldness of her last glance and had puzzled over it. That same coldness was in her manner now.

"Yes," she said stiffly.

The Kid paced his mount beside her wagon. "Didn't think I'd find *you* here," he remarked.

"This herd belongs to a half dozen Deadman spreads. Each outfit has a rep riding with it. I'm here for my dad's H-in-a-Hat."

The Kid grinned. "Storm Herndon's willin' to feed the railroad, eh?"

Her chin came up. "He made a bargain with Ty Whitman last fall," she said. "He's keeping that bargain. After that, he'll decide whether we sell more beef to the M.P. What do we want with a railroad on this range?"

"It'll get cattle to market without walkin' the tallow off 'em," the Kid observed. "It'll mean prosperity for the towns along the right-o-way."

"Like Caprock?" she mocked. "Is that your idea of what a town should be like? Drunken men and painted women?"

He shrugged. "I saw a sawbones operate on a man once," he said. "It wasn't pretty, but afterwards the gent was in better shape than he'd ever been."

She had no answer for that. Suddenly spurred by an

impulse, he swung from the saddle to the wagon seat, taking the reins from her hands before she could protest. "Miss Herndon," he said, "I wouldn't mind known' what there is about me that makes me look like a sidewinder to you."

"You don't know why?"

He shook his head.

She was silent for a thoughtful moment.

"Hellvation Hank was my friend," she said at last. "He always stopped at the H when he was in the Deadman country. He was a wonderful man. All he ever owned was the clothes he wore and the leather-bound Bible he carried, yet he was a lot happier than many men who measured themselves and each other by the acres they owned and the cattle they tallied. Can you understand that?"

"Hank," said the Kid, "was almost old enough to be my father. So I didn't know him well. He wrote me right often but I never saw him after I was a button."

"And you never worried about him, either," she snapped. "Yet Hellvation loved only two things—his work, and his kid brother. Oh, he told me all about you!"

"Must of been pretty," the Kid observed drily.

"It was as pretty as Hank could make it," she retorted. "But he was too honest to deny the truth. Young Matt was down on the Border. Matt was running wet cattle across the Rio. Matt was mixed up in some shirttail revolution and was smuggling guns into Mexico. Matt's name was linked with a bank robbery in the Panhandle. It seemed like Matt was in trouble most of the time."

She turned toward him.

"Can't you understand what you did to Hank? What it meant to him to have the brother he loved the kind of man who was everything Hank preached against and hated? Do you see that couldn't be any real happiness for Hank when he knew what you were? That's the cross Hellvation Hank carried. And you're the man who loaded it upon his shoulders!"

"But I'm here on account of him," he reminded her.

"Yes!" she blazed. "To shoot and to kill! That would be your way, Matt McGrath! I knew it when you spoke your piece to Tyler Whitman."

"Maybe Hellvation Hank wouldn't mind," he said, remembering things he'd read in his brother's Bible. "Didn't the Israelites have to get a mite rough with the Philistines before they won the Promised Land?"

The silence that fell between them was broken only by the bawling of the herd, the creak of the wagon.

"When a feller is young and headstrong he forgets a lot of things," the Kid finally remarked. "He forgets the mother who kept a lamp in the window for him, and the father who was stern because his own blood had been hot blood once. And he forgets the brother whose ways weren't his ways. But it's a long trail from Texas, and a man can do a heap of thinking on it."

He paused, his voice thick with suffering. "Then I began to savvy why patched britches and a four-dollar hoss was good enough for Hank," he said. "I'd have liked to told Hank about that when I got to Caprock. But you can't talk to a tombstone."

He turned at the pressure of her hand upon his arm and he was amazed to see tears jeweling her eyes.

"I—I'm sorry, Matt," she said. "I guess I forgot something, too—something about 'Judge not, lest ye be judged,' "

The Gospel Kid smiled, for it was as though a fence had been torn down between them. After that their talk turned to trivial things as the afternoon waned and dusk stole across the range.

Thunderheads were massing about the distant peaks and heat lightning played above the horizon when they made camp. Now the Kid had his first chance to meet the trail crew, five salty riders from as many different spreads. But the Kid did no more than acknowledge the introduction, for his interest was centered on the signs of a coming storm and his concern was for the bedded herd.

"I'll take the first watch," he volunteered.

• CHAPTER 8 •

THE GOSPEL KID, IN SADDLE AGAIN, RODE TOWARD the bedded herd, a darker bulk against the crowding darkness. Circling, he sang softly to them, humming his favorite toneless tune. A few drops of rain spattered against him and the sky growled a deep-voiced threat.

Yet the Kid knew a measure of contentment at this moment. Born to the saddle, he was doing his own kind of work once again. And he was remembering the half-forgotten dream of every wandering cowboy, the dream of a spread of his own and a herd to bear his brand.

But the Kid was also uneasy. For the feeling was strong upon him that the darkness cloaked forces which were no less potent because they weren't visible. There was something nameless out there in the night, something he felt but couldn't define. The cattle showed signs of restlessness, too, snorting irritably while horns rattled.

Minutes lengthened into an hour and deep darkness swathed the land as the Kid rode circle. A winking eye of fire had marked the distant camp where the weary riders slumbered, but now the fire had died away. The Kid's uneasiness became a clamoring presentiment of danger.

And then, as if in answer to his mood, rifles banged in the distance, barking from where the camp lay. Then suddenly the night was alive with riders, men who materialized out of the gloom with thundering guns. The raiders of the night swept down upon the far side of the herd, shouting and blazing away as they came.

Scared snorts became wild bellows as the cattle exploded into action. Instantly the herd was surging across the range in a mad stampede. And it the midst of it, a chip tossed by that torrent of fear-crazed beef, the Kid was swept along.

Ride the stampede! That was all the Kid could do. His long body flattened out over his mount's neck, he was carried forward by the fury of the herd's wild rush. It was dangerous enough to be swept along by the maddened beef but it would be certain death to try and check the crazed creatures.

Yet in the midst of peril the Kid's real fear was not for himself but for Lana Herndon. Guns in the distance meant the raiders were keeping the camp busy.

Who were those horsemen—hired guns of The Three, of Central Western, rustlers who had sighted prime beefs, theirs for the taking? Whoever they were, they had struck, and struck hard.

Thinking of Lana's peril goaded the Kid into making a desperate play. Reining carefully, he forced his horse toward the fringe of the herd. It was slow, nerve-racking work, for a single misstep might send horse and rider down beneath those thundering hoofs. Ahead was a bit of higher ground, and the Kid inched toward it. If he could gain that slight promontory, the herd might split and go around him. But the bluff seemed a million miles away and steers were still bolting past him as he angled toward it. Thirty feet . . . twenty . . . ten . . . In a few seconds he would be forcing his horse up the bluff, climbing to safety.

But that was when disaster overtook him. He never

knew how it happened. Maybe a gopher hole tripped his mount, maybe the horse lost its footing trying to dodge the raking horn of a fear-crazed steer. Whatever the cause, the horse suddenly stumbled and the Kid sailed over its head. He tried frantically to twist himself, to land on all fours. But the ground was rushing upward, a blinding light exploded before his eyes, and a greater darkness engulfed him. . . .

The lash of rain against his face brought the Kid back to consciousness and he found himself sprawled on sloping ground. He had reached the bluff after all. He lay there trying to coordinate his thoughts.

Lana! The herd! With the rush of memory he sat up, to find himself alone. Only the sibilant sound of the rain broke the silence and a flash of lightning revealed an endless vista of prairie, with no living thing in sight except his horse which stood nearby, reins trailing.

Apparently the mount hadn't been crippled by the fall. Painfully the Kid pulled himself into the saddle and rode toward the distant camp site. The wagon still stood there, and a cowboy sprawled, his sightless eyes staring into the sloppy heavens, a bullethole in his head. It wasn't the rain that chilled the Kid then. Lana was gone and so were the other four cowboys who had been hazing the herd.

Prisoners? It didn't make sense that the raiders would take prisoners. But the Deadman riders were gone, so the Kid headed in the direction the herd had been stampeded, hoping that somewhere he might find the missing.

Trailing wasn't easy for the rain had increased in its fury. But the sign was plain in the sodden ground although it would be washed away by morning if this storm continued. By cupping matches the Kid managed to assure himself that he was on the right trail. He had no way of knowing how long he had been unconscious, but he soon realized it couldn't have been long. The trail was fresh enough to prove that.

But most of the night was gone before a lightning

flash gave him a glimpse of the herd far ahead. He was overtaking it! Riders were hazing the spent cattle along, as he could see in the light that lasted for only a second before deeper darkness descended. The Kid's impulse was to put spurs to his horse, but he realized that caution might be his most potent weapon now.

He was beginning to recognize this country. He was nearing those palisading cliffs he had skirted the day before. They reared straight ahead, which meant the herd would have to angle either to the north or to the south.

The shallow stream which ran along the bottom of the cliffs had been whipped to a fury by the rain when the Kid stood on its bank a half hour later. Risking a match, he saw sign plain enough. The herd had been forced into the stream and the Kid, schooled along shadowy trails, smiled at the ancient ruse. The raiders were taking no chances. Let a wrathful posse of Deadman ranchers come riding in search of their vanished herd. Let them find sign. It would dead-end on the banks of this stream. Somewhere to the north or south the cattle would come to solid footing again.

Now the Kid could trail only by guesswork and there were two directions to take. He might have chosen one of them had not a sound reached him, one so faint as to be almost lost in the storm, yet recognizable. A shot! And he could have swom it came from directly across the stream!

His eyes strained, the Kid waited impatiently for the next lightning flash. It was slow in coming for the rain was beginning to abate. But the lightning came again, giving him a glimpse of the narrow strip of shore on the farther side. There was no place to hide a herd of cattle on that skimpy shelf, clogged with willows and bushes, with the cliffs rearing behind them. Yet the Kid forced his reluctant horse into the stream and, finding the water no more than belly-deep to the animal, he prodded the cayuse to the other shore.

And there, thrashing about among the dripping bushes on that narrow strip of land, he made another discovery—one that stiffened him in his saddle. These bushes had no roots. They had been piled here so as to appear natural to a casual eye on the opposite bank. But actually they were screening the mouth of a tunnel leading back under the cliff.

The Kid whistled low and tonelessly. A tunnel—a cleverly concealed tunnel! No wonder the herd had vanished. Probably a hundred other herds had vanished from the Deadman country in like fashion. With a storm to wash out sign, the raiders had the means of making cattle seemingly disappear from the face of the earth!

Out of saddle, the Kid cautiously edged into the tunnel, leading his horse. The silence of a tomb brooded in the place and the Kid risked a match or two. This was a natural tunnel. Probably the course of a subterranean river that had flowed here once had been changed by some upheaval of nature. The floor was dry and rocky, and the ceiling curved, never less than ten feet high, sometimes twice that height.

The tunnel was straight as an arrow, a faint glow marking its farther end. When the Kid emerged he found a rain-washed moon fighting to pierce the storm-scudded sky. The Kid passed a hand before his unbelieving eyes. Before him spread a valley, hidden behind the cliffs, a lush valley. And not half a mile away sprawled two cabins and a mammoth peeled-pole corral that held the snorting herd.

Here was a perfect hideout. Rustlers could hold beefs here as long as they chose, leisurely blotting brands before hazing them on to some dubious markets. Irate cattlemen could scour the range beyond the cliffs in vain.

But the Kid wasn't interested in cattle at this moment, nor in the possibilities this place afforded to those who knew its secret entrance. Where were Lana and the riders? Were they prisoners here? One of those cabins was dark and silent but light was showing from the windows of the others. Tying his horse in a clump of dripping bushes, the Kid eased toward the nearest window and raised his eyes above the sill.

In the glow of a flickering lamp on a split-log table he saw eight men inside. Eight big men and little men, on the faces of all the stamp of viciousness. They were talking as they discarded dripping garments. But the Kid didn't wait to try and hear what they were saying. These were the raiders, obviously. The Kid was interested in prisoners.

He crept toward the other cabin. It had only one small window, too small to allow the passage of a human body. The Kid heard restless movements inside and the faint murmur of voices. Scratching on the window sill, he ventured a whispered:

"Lana!"

The window swung inward. "Matt?" the girl whispered excitedly.

"You all right?" he asked. "And the boys? They in there?"

"All except Dave Woods of the Flying V. He was killed when the camp was attacked. Another of the boys was singed, but he isn't badly hurt."

"What's those snaky gents' game?" the Kid wanted to know. "Why did they fetch you here?"

"They didn't intend to," she said. "After the raid we took the trail after the rustlers. You were missing but we thought we'd find you trailing the herd, too. We followed them to the creek and we thought it was a good place to rush them. But they were too cagy for us. They prodded the herd into an amazing tunnel and ambushed us as we trailed after them. And we walked right into their trap! I managed to fire once before they had us covered."

"I heard the shot," the Kid said. Anger stirred as a new thought crossed his mind. "You shouldn't have taken that trail, girl. The boys shouldn't have let you take that trail."

"They didn't want to, Matt," she told him. "But what could they do? I'm representing the H, remember?"

• CHAPTER 9 •

SEEING NO POINT IN ARGUING A MATTER WHEN IT wouldn't change the situation, the Kid slipped to the door of the cabin, found it fastened by a heavy padlock and came back to report.

"I could blast it off with my gun," he said. "But the bunch in that other cabin would be on our necks pronto. It's too risky. Any ideas what they aim to do with your outfit?"

"I don't know," Lana admitted. "It looks bad, though, since we've learned the secret of this hideout. They can't let us walk off with that knowledge."

"It's beginning to get light," the Kid observed. "I'm duckin' for cover before they find me here. But I'll be close by and the minute they leave you alone I'll have that door open mighty fast."

He gave her his hand through the window and she gripped it, the four cowhands crowding behind her to whisper brief words of caution and advice. Then the Kid was blending with the shadows. Circling the cabin warily, he climbed to the lip of a cutbank overlooking the other cabin. Stretching himself prone, he waited.

It was a ticklish situation. Lana and the riders from the Deadman country had stumbled upon a secret which must have been jealousy guarded by rustlers for a long time. Yet even such hardcases as these would surely hesitate to kill a woman. But when the eight rustlers trooped out of the cabin in the first pale flush of dawn to stand ringed below him, the Kid had to admit that most of them looked capable of anything.

They were directly beneath him and the cutbank was no more than twelve feet high. He could throw a gun on them from here, hold them at bay and force them to fork over the key to the padlocked cabin. It would be risky, because the odds were eight to one. There was a strong chance that at least one of them would go for a gun, forcing a powdersmoke play.

That risk would have to be taken. If the Kid waited, they might leave long enough to give him time to get the prison cabin open, but they might not. Cautiously he eased his gun out of leather. That slight movement was his undoing. He had forgotten how close he was to the lip of the cutbank and he had forgotten that the rain might have weakened his precarious perch. The earth gave away with a sound like the crack of a gun. Clawing at the air, the Kid found himself tumbling downward in a shower of dirt and gravel, sprawling into the midst of those eight men below him.

A half dozen guns cleared holsters before the Kid lighted, and he sat up to find himself facing them. Now he was in a tight fix, and nobody knew it better than he did. His mind was racing desperately. It was bluff or die! The Kid managed to force a wry grin across his face.

"Some gents hallo a camp before they step in," he drawled cheerfully. "Me, I've got my own way of making noise."

"Just who the devil are you, mister?" snarled a

broad-faced, bearded man, who was almost as immense as Curly Bottsinger. "How did you get here?"

The Kid had expected to be greeted by gunfire but if they were willing to postpone his death even for a minute, he was certainly willing to accept the reprieve.

"South is my name," he said. "Dusty South. I caught a glimpse of you gents pushing your beef herd through a wall—a rock wall. 'Dusty,' I sez, 'either you're loco or full of forty-rod busthead. It ain't natural for cow critters to walk through a wall,' I got so plumb curious I trailed along."

"A curious gent, eh?" the big man growled.

A lean, snaky gent whose face seemed to be mostly nose sidled up.

"He's one of 'em, Cisco," he said. "He's a Deadman waddy we didn't bag last night!"

"I ain't so sure," big Cisco argued. "I studied the crew through glasses yesterday morning. There was five cowhands and the girl. You salivated one of them cowhands. One of 'em was holdin' the herd but he got caught in the stampede during the raid. We got four of 'em and the girl here, ain't we? That makes this jigger a stray." He pinned a glance on the Kid. "Where's your horse?"

"Yonder in the bushes," the Kid confessed without hesitation.

"Take a look-see at its brand you, Shark Lund," Cisco ordered and the big-nosed man hurried to obey. He was back quickly. "A bay with a brand I never saw before, Yawberry," he reported reluctantly. "It ain't from the Deadman range."

"Where do you hail from, mister?" "Cisco" Yawberry demanded.

The Kid grinned. "Now I ain't askin' you no questions," he reminded. "Can't a gent keep his backtrail to himself?"

* * *

It was like teetering on the edge of a volcano, and the Kid wondered how long it would last. But he was still alive, a miracle in itself, for these hardcases had the look of men who might have killed him first and asked questions afterward. It was the very boldness of his attitude that was his saving. He had aroused their curiosity, and perhaps their grudging admiration. The Kid pursued his brash policy with an assurance he was far from feeling.

"Do I smell coffee boilin' in that *cabana*?" he asked. "I'd shore like some."

He was studying the rustlers all the while. He had seen a thousand faces along the Montana-Pacific's right-of-way, and he couldn't know whether he'd seen these eight before. Also, he couldn't be sure whether they'd ever seen him or not. But he had been at end o' steel most of this last month and he was certain this crew hadn't been among the workers, so sure that he was gambling on it. And he was winning, for Cisco Yawberry pouched his gun.

"Fetch him a cup of coffee," the rustler chief ordered.

Squatting crosslegged, the Kid took the steaming cup when it was handed to him. One by one, the men dropped to the ground, forming a semicircle facing him. Following Yawberry's cue, all the rustlers had leathered their irons but they were eyeing the Kid warily, especially the snaky, big-nosed man who answered to the name Shark Lund.

The Kid knew how fragile was this spell he had cast by his apparent fearlessness. By his own admission, he had trailed them here. What was more to the point, he possessed dangerous knowledge—the secret of that tunnel which served them so well. That made him just as much of a menace to their security as those five prisoners who knew of this hideout. Chances were his fate would be the same as theirs.

The Kid decided on the most desperate bluff of all—a bluff that would shorten his life to a span of a second if it were called. He cursed and reached for his gun, speaking swiftly. The outcome of this play was going to depend on how fast he could talk, rather than on how fast he could unlimber his gun.

"You're not collecting Montana-Pacific head money on me!" he snarled. "I ain't bein' taken alive, savvy!"

He had moved so swiftly as to catch them unawares and though he had wrenched his gun from leather he might have died then. There were eight of them and at least one of them could have got him. But they stared open-mouthed.

"Montana-Pacific head money!" Cisco Yawberry echoed. "You sayin' the railroad's got a price on you?"

"Don't stall!" the Kid spat. "You know well enough it has! You're aimin' on packin' my pelt to Tyler Whitman. I could see it in the eyes of every blasted one of you as you watched me!"

"What's Whitman want you for?" Yawberry demanded.

"You're bluffin'." The Kid laughed. "You know I'm the gent who put a bullet through that long-geared Texas troubleshooter of M.P.'s in Lazura the other day."

"McGrath! Heard tell of him. You killed that gent!"

"As dead as he's ever goin' to be!" the Kid snarled.

Yawberry grinned broadly. "Put away your gun, Dusty," he advised the Kid. "You got us plumb wrong. See that herd yonder? That's beef Montana-Pacific had a notion it was goin' to eat."

His ruse had worked!

That was the Kid's triumphant thought but in the midst of it he knew an almost overpowering temptation. He had this crew under his gun. Why not force the play through as he had planned before the cutbank had caved? Why not make them release the prisoners? He realized, though, that there was such a thing as pushing luck too far. Besides, he had just paved the way for a better opportunity.

"Rustlers, eh?" The Kid grinned as he pouched his gun. "I sort of figured that. But the way you gents kept lookin' at me, I wasn't sure how you stood."

"You're among friends," Yawberry assured him. "Any gent that's had the snake sign put on him by M.P. can ride with this outfit."

"Just a minute, Cisco," Shark Lund put in. "I ain't so shore about this jigger. It's for the boss to say whether he's all right or not, savvy?"

Cisco bristled belligerently.

"Well, he's stayin' here until the boss shows up—tonight or tomorrow. The boss can decide what we'll do with them Deadman cowhands, too, and he can size up Dusty here. But I'm thinkin' he'll sign up this salty gent pronto."

The Kid hadn't hoped to win them all over but Yawberry, who appeared to be in command, had accepted him. But the real chief of this outfit would be along shortly, and the doom of the prisoners would be sealed. Meantime, the Kid still had his gun.

It was the beginning of the longest day in the Gospel Kid's life. He spent the greater part of it squatting in the shadow of the cabin, shaping cigarettes endlessly and spinning windies with the rest. He had a part to play, and he played it well. He might have been as ruthless as any of them, according to his yarns. Shark Lund watched him covertly but the Kid paid the big-nosed man no heed. And before noon came even Lund was less frigid.

A pockmarked little man whose swarthy skin betrayed his mixed blood cooked a meal. Afterwards the man took food to the other cabin. The Kid watched him indolently as the fellow fished a key from a pocket, unpadlocked the door and, gun in hand, slid the food inside. The door was immediately locked again.

It was the Kid's hope that something would take the rustler crew away during the afternoon. If they left, he would have to go with them, he knew, but he might be able to slip away long enough to return and release the prisoners. But as the hours dragged on, the eight men still loitered about, plainly intending to do nothing. The corraled cattle weren't even turned loose to graze or taken to water, and their irritable bawling became nerve-racking.

Some of the rustler mended bridles, hunkering near a pile of gear stacked beside a makeshift corral which held the horses of the prisoners and their captors. One rustler whittled lazily while two others stretched themselves upon the ground, their sombreros tilted over their noses, and snatched some sleep during the heat of the day.

Convinced that no opportunity would present itself while there was daylight, the Kid also took a nap. He was dead tired, and might need renewed strength before another sunup.

• Chapter 10 •

Wearily the day passed, and dusk came at last to purple this hidden valley. Felipe, the cook, stirred himself to activity only after being urged profanely, but it was dark before supper was eaten. As before, Felipe headed then for the other cabin.

The Kid came to his feet, yawning and stretching, his apparent indolence giving no hint of his inner excitement. The time had come to force a play. A lamp had been lighted in the cabin and a poker game was claiming the attention of most of the rustlers. For a moment the Kid, left alone, stalked boldly toward the other cabin. He met Felipe, returning.

"It ees loco, senior," Felipe observed with a flash of white teeth. "Why should I feed thees hombres when tomorrow we keel them perhaps?"

"It's shore crazy," the Kid agreed, and laid his gun barrel across Felipe's head.

The man went down without a moan. Instantly the Kid was pawing into the cook's pockets, and when he sprinted toward the dark prison cabin, the key was in his hands. He thought he heard hoofs drumming in the distance, but there wasn't time to be concerned about anything but the job ahead.

He got the door open quickly.

"Lana!" he called. "It's me—Matt!"

She came to him at once. "Matt!" she exclaimed thankfully.

"You've got to work fast," he whispered. "I can't stay here long or I'll be missed. You and the boys slip out and get gear onto horses. I'll meet you as soon as I can, and we'll make a break for it!"

A voice was raised in the darkness. "Dusty! Dusty South! Where in thunder are you? Cisco wants you!"

"I've got to go," the Kid panted. "I'll see what Cisco wants and stall him. You do as I told you."

He slid away, stepping over unconscious Felipe, a shapeless huddle in the darkness. There was a prayer in the heart of the Kid that Felipe would stay unconscious for quite a while, and wouldn't be missed. The Kid walked boldly toward the lighted cabin and big Cisco Yawberry was waiting for him just outside the door.

"Step inside, Dusty," Yawberry said. "The boss is here. Come on in and speak your own piece to him."

The Kid remembered those drumming hoofbeats. So the rustler chief had arrived. That complicated things. But he had to stall all of them, the boss included, until Lana and the Deadman cowboys were in saddles. So the Kid stepped into the cabin, to stare slackjawed at the man who awaited him. And if there was amazement in the Kid's eyes, it was mirrored doubly in the eyes of the man he faced. For the boss of this rustling crew was—Hoyt Durham!

Of all the thoughts that flashed through the mind of the Gospel Kid as he faced the man here in this rustlers' lair, two were predominant. Durham's presence here definitely branded the man as one of The Three. Durham, the leader of these night-riding raiders, proved Durham was battling the Montana-Pacific for his own selfish gain. And the game of bluff was over. He couldn't fool Durham. The saloon man knew him, had tried to have him killed in Caprock.

All the outlaws were here in the cabin, except Felipe. Most of the men sat around the table where cards were spread in the kerosene lamp's glow. The instant Durham spoke the pack would be on the Kid.

But he didn't wait for Durham to find his tongue. Instead he kicked over the table and his fist lashed Durham as the table crashed and the lamp went out, leaving the room in darkness. He heard Durham sprawl across the wrecked table and heard men curse as they were pinned beneath the wreckage. Then the Kid was through the doorway.

He had forced the play and had gained the advantage of surprise. No man except Durham had expected him to make a hostile move and even Durham had been unprepared for the Kid's lightning attack. The Kid swung the door shut behind him but instead of bolting into the darkness he grasped the crude door handle and braced one foot against the wall to hold the door shut.

"Lana," he shouted. "Pile into saddles and get! Hell's busted loose!"

Cursing men were tugging at the door from the inside. There were eight of them, providing Durham hadn't been knocked unconscious, but no more than one or two could get their hands on the small inside handle at the same time. They couldn't combine their strength against the Kid's. But one of the rustlers, cooler-headed than the others, was driving bullets through the door, the lead smashing dangerously close to the Gospel Kid. And sooner or later someone was going to climb through a window. All the Kid could hope to do was to stall them for a few more precious minutes.

A rider flashed by him—Lana Herndon.

"Up!" she shouted, and the Kid saw other riders, the Deadman cowhands, fanning wide. He let the door go then, firing twice into the dark interior of the shack as the door swung inward. That lead stopped the first rush of men outside and the Kid swung up behind Lana.

"Got to get my own horse!" the Kid panted. "Can't ride double and outrun 'em!"

But Lana had ideas of her own and suddenly the Kid saw the shape of them when she loped, not toward the distant tunnel, but straight toward the corraled beef herd. The riders with her were already there and one of them was snaking the corral gate open. The cattle, hungry and thirsty and irritable, charged into the open, the riders whooping and slapping sombreros against their chaps as they spread to flank them.

The herd needed no urging. The cattle smelled water and bolted in the direction. The rustlers' cabin was directly in the path of the herd. The Kid saw Lana's strategy then. With a wild shout, he fired a couple of shots to add to the bedlam just as a half dozen shadowy figures poured from the cabin.

Those rustlers stopped in their tracks when they found themselves facing that oncoming avalanche of beef. With shrill yells of terror they dashed back into the cabin, as anxious to get inside again as they had been to get out. One of them tripped, went down, came to his feet again—too late. The Kid had a brief glimpse of the fear-twisted face of Shark Lund, saw the man's upflung arms, then Lund vanished, lost beneath a waving, tossing sea of horns as the herd split, surging around the cabin where the other rustlers cowered.

The Deadman crew had turned all of the horses out of the corral and the mounts of the rustlers were swept along by the herd. Behind the racing animals came the Kid and those he had rescued. When they reached the inner mouth of the tunnel the six in saddles sweated to force the fringes of the herd into the cavern. Once that was done, in half an hour the herd was scattered along the stream, drinking their fill. The Kid sat his saddle, gun in hand, his eye on the tunnel's mouth. But none of the rustlers put in an appearance. Shortly the herd was rounded up and headed on the trail.

"Might just as well push 'em on tonight," the Kid decided. "We don't have to worry about those galoots back there. They can't catch us without horses. There's no use tryin' to go back and round up those gents, either. They've got guns a-plenty and we've got one between the bunch of us."

But first they angled to the site of their camp of the night before. And there, on the spot where Dave Woods had died, they buried the valiant Flying V puncher. The Kid read from Hellvation Hank's Bible in the first light of the rising moon, the others standing bareheaded around the shallow grave.

Dawn found them at the camp of the Montana-Pacific's tunnel builders. The Kid thought of rounding up some of the crew and heading back to the hidden valley to round up Yawberry's bunch but decided that would be futile. With the valley's location no longer a secret, the rustlers would hightail from the hideout as fast as feet could carry them.

Lana had gone to a tent to snatch a few hours sleep. When she arose at noon the herd was gone, already headed out for the end of steel, and the Kid waiting for her.

"You're going back to the H-in-a-Hat," he told her firmly. "I'll rep for your dad when the beef's paid for. You've done enough trail drivin'."

She didn't argue. If the smile she gave him was wan, it was also appreciative.

Within an hour they were loping across the rangeland toward the distant H-in-a-Hat, two pygmy figures in that vast stretch of prairie.

* * *

As they rode along they talked mostly of Hellvation Hank, for the Kid was hungry for details about the brother he had scarcely known.

"You're so different from him—yet like him, too," Lana said. "Last night, when we buried poor Dave, you might have been Hank. You could hang up your gun and be a sky-pilot, Matt."

He smiled. "I've studied the Bible a heap," he admitted. "But that was to read some meaning into a message Hank left behind him. It's a queer yarn—"

And then he was telling her the whole story of how he had received that bloodstained Bible and had gradually come to understand the significance of the marked references. He told her how he had taken the trail to the north then, and he told her of what he had learned since he'd gone to work for the railroad.

"Goliath, Herod and Judas," he concluded thoughtfully. "I'm sure, now, that Bottsinger is Goliath, for they tell me he stands to lose a heap when the railroad offers a cheaper service to take the place of his highway-robbin' freight line. Hoyt Durham is Herod. If I'd had any doubts, they went up in smoke when Durham showed up last night. But Judas is the gent I've still got to cut sign on."

"And when you do?" she ventured.

"Like you said—I'm different from Hank," he reminded her, and something in the way he said it made her drop the subject.

• CHAPTER 11 •

DUST WAS STEALING ACROSS THE RANGELAND WHEN the Gospel Kid and Lana Herndon reached the H-in-a-Hat, a cluster of buildings cupped in a verdant coulee to shelter them from the winds of winter. This H-in-a-Hat was a cowman's dream, the Kid thought. There could be no better ending to any trail than such a spread as this.

"There's Dad on the porch!" the girl cried excitedly.

"Storm" Herndon was seated in a rocker on the long porch that fronted the ranchhouse and in the graying twilight the Kid could see the rancher. He was anxious to meet Storm Herndon, for he had heard enough about the salty old cattleman to know he was going to like him. But gazing at this sturdy oldster with his seamed, leathery face, with a ragged rim of gray hair fringing a semi-bald head, the Kid stiffened in his saddle.

"We've met before, haven't we?" the Kid said quietly.

"Dad!" Lana cried "This is—"

Storm Herndon had half-risen from his chair but he settled back again, his eyes aflame as he glared at the Kid, and something about his wild look locked the tongue of his daughter.

"Get out!" Herndon suddenly roared. "Get off this place! Do you savvy? Before I put a slug into you!"

Lana gazed in bewilderment from one man to the other.

"Dad! You don't understand. This man—"

"It's you that don't savvy," her father raged. "But you'll hate this jigger as much as I do when you get the straight of it. Now get, mister—fast!"

The girl's eyes swung toward the Kid and the anguish in them held his tongue.

"Never mind," was all he said before he touched spurs to his horse, rode out of the ranch yard, and turned his back upon the man he had fought in Crowfoot Gulch the night he had witnessed the dynamiting of the trestle, the man he had last seen rolling down the slope of the gulch!

He heard Lana call him, but he paid no heed. He wanted to put distance between himself and the H-in-a-Hat. There was plenty to think about!

Storm Herndon—dynamiter! That didn't make sense. Yet the rancher had been in the gulch that night and he had flared up at the sight of the Kid, the one man who knew he had been there. That cinched the rancher's guilt, but the Kid didn't want to believe the obvious. Still, Tyler Whitman himself had warned that Herndon might not be an ally. "He hates the railroad and makes no bones about it," Whitman had said. "If Herndon gets it into his head to buck the road, he'll fight hard . . ."

Did Herndon hate the railroad so much that he was using any means to fight it? It looked like it. Herndon was a diehard who wanted to cling to the old days and the old ways. But his daughter had been on the train which would have plunged into Crowfoot Gulch if the

Kid hadn't stopped it. Had Herndon known Lana was on that train?

And what about the fact that hired outlaws of The Three had run off a beef herd belonging to Deadman ranchers? That herd had been jointly owned by six spreads. Had Herndon included his own cattle to keep suspicion from himself? Had he allowed his daughter to go with the herd, knowing that no matter how much lead might be scattered, she would not be hurt? She had appeared to be in danger of her life in the hidden valley. But where was the proof that she actually had been in peril? Perhaps she would have been spared, not because she was a woman, but because she was Storm Herndon's girl.

There was much the Kid didn't know, but there were certainly signs that Storm Herndon might be betraying the other ranchers, and betraying his friend, Tyler Whitman.

But there was no indication that Lana was aware of her father's perfidy. The Kid found some consolation in that as he wrestled with the problem across the lonely miles.

He was no nearer a solution when he unlimbered himself from his saddle in Lazura the next day. His first duty was to report to Tyler Whitman, but instead he went to the telegraph office. Key O'Dade had been moved from Caprock to this new boom-town and the squat Irishman was at his instrument.

"Look," said the Kid. "Can you dig something out of the records for me? I've got to know if Storm Herndon got a wire from his girl in April, a wire saying she'd be coming to Caprock on a certain train."

O'Dade scratched his head.

"Shure and this is a railroad telegraph. Sich wires as we send for other folks is for the promotin' of good will. There's no record of thim, bhoy."

"But can't you remember?" the Kid asked desperately. "Think hard!"

O'Dade's face corrugated with the effort. "I'm thinkin' there was no sich wire, but it's no oath I'll be takin' on it,'' he decided. ''No, bhoy, I can't tell yez for sure.''

The Kid turned into the clamorous street, his face grim. There was nothing to dispel the black shadow of suspicion that clouded his mind. All signs said Storm Herndon was an enemy of the railroad, a far more ruthless enemy than he claimed to be, a betrayer of his neighbors and his friends—a Judas!

It looked as though the Kid had found his third man. But where was the satisfaction in that when the man was Lana's father?

The steel reached Deadman the second week in July, rejuvenating the torpid town. With hammers pounding day and night, a score of buildings blossomed to lengthen the false-fronted street. Deadman had accented the heritage of turmoil bequeathed by a dying Lazura and a dead Caprock.

On the last day of July the rails were twenty miles beyond Deadman and the Big Thunders echoed to the clang of sledge against spike and the puffing of the work trains. The Montana-Pacific's first tunnel had passed the beginning of the mountain barrier without a wasted day.

The Kid was always at end o' steel. Under the blistering sun he was everywhere and anywhere, sometimes pumping a handcar up and down the right-of-way, alert for trouble that never materialized, sometimes swinging a sledge or lending a hand when the track layers deposited the shining steel upon the ladder of ties.

He was a troubled man: a man whose waking hours were a torture, and who worked ceaselessly so that he might sleep and forget when night came. He grew lean and morose and his easy grin was gone. There was no enthusiasm in him, even though each day brought victory nearer and rumor whispered that the Central Western was so far behind as to be almost out of the race.

When the Kid had come back after the delivery of the beef herd, his report to Whitman had been brief.

''We got the herd through,'' he had said. ''Had some

trouble with rustlers. Hoyt Durham was the head of those wideloopers. Herndon's girl was reppin' for her dad but I chased her home."

"I'll send Herndon's money to him by one of the Deadman cowboys," Whitman had promised, then arched his brows thoughtfully. "Looks like Durham's one of The Three, eh? The tough part is that we can't do a thing to him. When there isn't any law you can't arrest a man. And even if we could, it would be your word against his. But at least we know he's an enemy. I can hit him where it'll hurt the worse—in his pocketbook. I'll post an order that no M.P. man is to patronize his place. If you run into Durham, you can use your own judgment what to do."

It was all that was ever said about the matter but that was the reason for the Kid's turmoil. It was his duty to tell Whitman the whole story, including his suspicions concerning Storm Herndon. And it was the Kid's duty—to himself—to force a showdown with Hoyt Durham. But he didn't run into the man, or Curly Bottsinger either, for the simple reason that the Kid chose to avoid the pair—and hated himself for doing it.

He was beaten—beaten by a slip of a girl. But he was honest enough to face the fact. He had sworn to kill three men—Goliath and Herod and Judas. One was as guilty as the others, yet if his torturing suspicions were true, how could he kill Lana Herndon's father? And what could he say before the tribunal of his own conscience if he wreaked vengeance upon Durham and Bottsinger and spared the third man?

That was why the Kid worked like a demon from morning to night, until he began to sense that a man may move swiftly, but never so fast that he can escape from himself. But still he toiled on with the heart gone out of him until Tyler Whitman, misunderstanding, called him aside on that last day of July.

"Are you trying to build this railroad singlehanded, Matt?" he chided. "There's a limit to what one man can do, but you don't seem to realize it. The trouble seems to be all over, and you've earned a rest. Take a couple days off and go to Deadman and have some fun. That's an order, understand?''

The Kid didn't argue. There was no lure for him in Deadman but he took the work train back to town, finding the blackness of the tunnel enroute no darker than his mood. He alighted, swung along another clamorous street, seeing the same signs that had adorned Caprock and Lazura, hearing the same barkers shouting from a dozen saloon doorways. He swung past the tent housing Thackery Weaver's *End O' Steel Echo*, quickening his pace, for he was in no frame of mind to listen to the garrulous editor. He turned into the Palace Hotel for want of a better place to spend his time.

The room he was given overlooked the alley and the Kid sat before the window, staring out with brooding eyes, the clamor of the street beating against him as it rose from the distance. He got an idea of going on a good toot, and was annoyed to find that such an inspiration no longer held any allure for him. And while he sat there, wrapped in gloomy thought, he saw a figure steal surreptitiously down the alleyway below and recognized the gaunt, seedy-looking man—Shadow Loomis.

The Kid's interest quickened. He had never got any more than within shouting distance of Shadow Loomis since that day in Caprock when he had bought liquor for for the man—which Loomis had poured into a cuspidor. But the Kid had thought of Loomis often and had wanted to talk to him. So now the Gospel Kid swung a leg over the window sill, dropped to the roof of a low shed flanking the rear of the hotel, and leaped to the ground. Loomis was angling out of the alley when the Kid next glimpsed the man and he followed silently and swiftly.

The trail of Shadow Loomis was a sinuous one and sometimes the Kid was hard put to keep him in sight. But he managed and was still trailing when Loomis scuttled into a small shack on the outskirts of the town, a sagging-roofed shack so decrepit-looking as to be a fitting abode for the dissolute man. Was this where Loomis lived? When the Kid pressed an ear to the outer wall he heard only the slight movements of one man inside.

The Kid opened the door without knocking and stepped inside.

A crude table, a few crippled chairs, a cot and a rusty stove furnished the single room. Loomis was seated behind the table, and just for an instant astonishment crossed his face as he recognized the Kid. Then his eyes became as bleary-looking as ever and his voice held its familiar whining note.

"What you doing here?" he demanded with a show of truculence.

"I've come for a palaver," said the Kid, "and I ain't in a mood to mess with words. Just who in blazes are you—and what's your game?"

"Game?" Loomis countered, half-cringing. "I'm just a gent that's down on his luck. I'm not making trouble for anybody."

"That's all you've got to say?"

"That's all," Loomis quavered.

The Kid swept the table aside with a brush of his hand and he was upon Loomis in the same motion, his fingers gripping the man's stringy throat.

"Talk, curse you!" the Kid gritted. "Talk up—and fast! You've followed the steel all the way from Cap-rock. You sneak and you snoop, and you're always around. Mister, maybe you're one of The Three. You've got a lot of explainin' to do. Start talkin'!"

• CHAPTER 12 •

LOOMIS, GASPING, MANAGED TO SPEAK.

"The Three!" he spluttered. "You figure I'm—"

"I don't know," the Gospel Kid said truthfully, for suddenly he was a little ashamed of his own belligerence.

This seedy-looking individual was a man of mystery, all right, but where was the proof that he was also a man of evil? The Kid realized that he, himself, was clutching at straws, looking in vain for another Judas, when he had already found the real one.

"Wait!" Loomis cried. "I'll show you how wrong you are!"

He scurried to his cot and dragged something from beneath it.

"Look!" he said. "Do you still think I'm on *their* side of the fence?"

"Another one!" the Kid exclaimed, and all of the doubt left him as Loomis held aloft a pine headboard much like the one the Kid had seen in Dan Callishaw's room back in Caprock. The lettering read:

HERE LIES S. LOOMIS
DIED AUGUST 15, 18—
HIS EARS WAS TOO BIG FOR THE
SIZE OF HIS HEAD

"August fifteenth!" the Kid said. "Shucks, man, that's only a couple of weeks away! Just why have they put the deadwood on you?"

Loomis thrust the headboard out of sight and, as he regarded the Kid thoughtfully, the bleariness went out of his eyes and his shoulders straightened.

"Maybe I'd better tell you the truth," he decided, and even his voice had changed. "They're after me because they suspect what I really am. Here—feel."

He took the Kid's hand, pressing it against his shabby corduroy coat and the Kid felt the bulge of something sewed inside the lining.

"Government credentials," Loomis explained.

The Kid's eyes widened. "A Government man! Doing what?"

"Keeping an eye on the race between the M.P. and the C.W. The Government has promised to subsidize the first road to cross the Big Thunders. A bond issue and a gift of a couple hundred feet of right-of-way on both sides of the rails isn't to be sneezed at. But the Government wants the race to be fair. I'm here to watch."

"But why didn't you let us know?" the Kid demanded. "Why didn't you tell Whitman, or Kurt Ormond?"

"I was told to work incognito, playing whatever role I saw fit. I came to Caprock last fall, pretending to be a sort of drunken remittance man. That's how I met up with Hellvation Hank."

"You knew Hank?"

Loomis smiled wryly. "Knew him? He tried to save me from what he thought I was! He worked hard to keep me away from the whisky I appeared to be drinking. Yes, I knew him—and respected him highly. It was to Hank that I first spoke of The Three—something I had no business doing. But the railroad meant a lot to Hank."

The Kid was all excitement. "You know who The Three are?" he demanded.

"I know the identity of two of them," Loomis admitted. "Since I'm pretty sure the M.P. also knows, there isn't any reason why I shouldn't speak the names of Durham and Bottsinger. I don't know who the third man is. But Hank did some snooping himself, and he learned the whole truth, somehow, for he told me so. 'Come to church and maybe you'll hear all three names,' he told me. That night he died."

"But you've got your suspicions," the Kid said bluntly. "I'm askin' you, as one man to another, is Storm Herndon tied up with The Three?"

"I don't know," Loomis said. "Once I managed to search Durham's private office, but I couldn't find a thing to implicate anybody. Herndon was in Caprock last fall, though, and this spring too. Nobody's talked more against the railroad than he has. If I was troubleshooter for M.P., McGrath, I'd have a plain talk with him."

"You're dead right!" the Kid said slowly. "And I'm going to do it—pronto."

He extended his hand, a ghost of his old grin crossing his face.

"I'm sorry I mussed you up," he said. "Take care of yourself. When those boys send out those timber tombstones, they're not jokin'."

"I know it," Loomis said soberly. "I'm going to hole up in the Big Thunders for a couple of weeks. So long, McGrath. Keep what I've told you under your hat. The information was for Hank McGrath's brother, not for the M.P. troubleshooter."

"They're two different fellows—sometimes," the Kid conceded gravely and left.

His destination was miles away—the H-in-a-Hat spread. He was going to have a showdown with Storm Herndon. The very fact of having made the decision lifted some of the load he had been shouldering. But before he left Deadman he went to the railroad office to see if there were any new orders. Key O'Dade greeted him gravely.

"Faith and it was looking for ye, I was," the Irishman said. "This wire came from Whitman for ye. 'Tis bad news, me bhoy, bad news."

The Kid ran his eye over the slip Whitman had wired:

WATCH YOUR BACK. HEADBOARD SIMILAR TO ONE SENT CALLISHAW FOUND IN YOUR TENT. NAMES AUGUST SECOND AS DAY OF YOUR DEATH.

"August second," the Kid mused, as he balled the slip in his fist. "Time enough to get to the H-in-a-Hat anyway."

In ten minutes he was swinging aboard a work train headed for end o' steel . . .

The Golden Slipper Saloon was in Deadman now with the dying of Lazura, a more substantial layout since it was rumored that Deadman might enjoy a boom until the spring. But though prepared to continue reaping a golden harvest, the Golden Slipper was a silent, gloomy place, for Tyler Whitman's word was law and the M.P. men shunned Hoyt Durham's establishment.

The blacklisting had been a bitter blow for Durham. Disgust was in his swarthy face as he sat in his private office situated, as usual, behind "The Lady of the Nile." A black mood was upon Curly Bottsinger, too.

"McGrath headed back for end o' steel," he reported. "One of the boys saw him catch the train. But that wooden warning ain't goin' to scare that gent! We're wastin' our time scarin' small fry like Shadow Loomis, too."

The third man was in a buoyant mood and he smiled expansively.

"If Loomis is what I think he is, he isn't small fry," he observed. "If I'm wrong, what difference does it make what happens to a barfly? I don't expect the headboard to scare McGrath into running, but it will probably keep him out at end o' steel for the next couple of days. He won't be in Deadman to smell a rat when things begin to happen."

Hoyt Durham was the first to understand what he meant, and suddenly the saloon owner was smiling eagerly.

"You mean you're ready to pull the big act?" he demanded. "The time has come for the real showdown?"

"Exactly. Cisco Yawberry and his bunch will be in town just as soon as they finish that little business out on the Deadman range. And everybody else is ready, since we've planned this for weeks. No slipups, remember! It's got to work like a clock!"

He poured himself a drink from Durham's private bottle, as did the other two, hoisting their glasses together.

"To the downfall of the Montana-Pacific," toasted the third man. "And to the greater glory of the Central Western."

"To the hell that's goin' to be turned loose!" Bottsinger added darkly, and downed his drink in a single gulp . . .

The Gospel Kid, on his way to the H-in-a-Hat spread, rode the work train to the end of the tracks. He burned with a desire to see Herndon, to rid himself of his festering suspicions, or to force the old rancher to show his hand. But first the Kid wanted to see Tyler Whitman. He found the railroad builder in his private coach on a siding.

"I'm glad you came back!" Whitman said, with a worried frown. "One of the boys poked into your tent for something and found that headboard I wired you about. I'd like to think it's a bluff, Matt, but I'm not so sure. They weren't bluffing when they sent the same warning to Dan Callishaw."

Whitman produced the headboard. The lettering read:

HERE LIES MATTHEW MCGRATH
BORN JANUARY 1, 18—
DIED AUGUST 2, 18—
HE WAS LUCKY—BUT HIS
LUCK RAN OUT

The Kid scarcely gave it a glance.

"I'm quitting the railroad," he told Whitman. "No, I'm not runnin' out on account of that headboard. It's just like I told Kurt Ormond once—I've got two jobs to do. One was working for the railroad. I said if it ever happened I had to take care of the other job first, I'd leave the railroad. Looks like now I've got some business of my own to tend to—important business. I'm takin' a little pasear across the range."

Whitman regarded him thoughtfully.

"Have it your way, boy," he decided at last. "I'll ask no questions. And I'll feel better if you're somewhere else for a spell. But I want you to know that we've got a place for you here whenever you finish this other job of yours. And be careful!"

Ten minutes after they'd shaken hands the Kid was in saddle, following the rails back through the tunnel and beyond it, then angling northward. He made a fireless camp when night overtook him not far from the cliffs that barricaded the hidden valley. Most of the day his mind had been upon what might happen at the end of this trail. It wasn't until he was stretched upon his saddle blanket, studying the stars and smoking a last cigarette, that it came to him with something of a start that his birth date as lettered on the headboard had been the correct date.

That was queer. Dan Callishaw's birth date had been correct, too, but Callishaw had given information to Thackery Weaver which the editor had used in his newspaper write-up about Callishaw. Callishaw's birth date had become public knowledge.

On the other hand, Loomis' headboard had mentioned no birth date. But Loomis, seemingly a barfly, wouldn't be in the list of names and data Thackery Weaver had kept, the list the editor had claimed had been stolen.

But no man from Caprock to the Big Thunders had known the birth date of Matt McGrath, save Hellvation Hank. And Hank was dead. The Kid went to sleep trying to solve the riddle.

With morning he gave it no further thought. The miles were unreeling behind him and he was nearing the lush coulee that sheltered the H-in-a-Hat buildings. And his mind once more was only on what he had to say to Storm Herndon when he faced that fiery cattleman.

• Chapter 13 •

Below the ranchhouse, the trail dipped into the coulee where the ravine was narrower and riotous with rose briars, serviceberry bushes, and a few scraggy fir trees. The shrubbery formed a screen of sorts.

The Gospel Kid rounded a turn to find himself facing an approaching rider. His heart leaped. It was Lana, in levis and jumper and floppy sombrero.

For a silent moment they faced each other as each jerked to a halt.

"Matt!" Lana cried then. "You've come back!" Something in his face made her voice falter.

"I've come to see your father, Lana," he said. "Maybe you can guess why. But tell me one thing first, Lana—something I've *got* to know. Did you wire him you were coming to Caprock by train last spring?"

"No, I didn't. I was coming home against his orders. I . . . Oh, I see what you're driving at! That dynamiting in Crowfoot Gulch. Matt, there was such a ghastly misunderstanding about that! After Dad drove you off the place, I demanded that he explain and he did.''

"I'm listenin'," the Kid said woodenly.

"Dad was in Caprock that night and he happened to see a bunch of riders head out of town leading a pack-horse with a box of dynamite loaded on it. He thought Curly Bottsinger was heading the outfit, but he wasn't sure. The more he thought about it, the more he wondered what Bottsinger intended doing with dynamite along the railroad right-of-way. Bottsinger hated the railroad because it meant the finish of his freight line. Dad hated the railroad too, but he couldn't stomach underhanded fighting. He fretted about it until he decided to follow those riders. He trailed them to Crowfoot Gulch. He left his horse and crept to a ledge for a better look, but got there too late. He just barely had time to shelter himself behind an outcropping of rocks when the blast went off."

"I savvy," said the Kid, but there was skepticism in his voice.

"But you don't!" she countered. "Dad recognized you as the man who'd jumped him in the gulch. All he could do that night was fight back. He thought *you* were one of the dynamiters. Do you wonder that he flew into a rage when he saw you again?" Her lips quivered. "I'll always remember what you said when I thanked you for saving our lives. 'I just happened along,' you said. 'It might have been anybody!' Dad just happened along, too. Doesn't that entitle him to the benefit of the doubt?"

"It does," the Kid conceded. "And yet the whole thing is too pat—too pat. He claims to be Ty Whitman's friend in spite of their difference of opinion about the railroad. Why didn't he tell Whitman about the explosion?"

"He couldn't even be positive it was Bottsinger he'd seen," she said wearily. "Besides, you don't understand Dad's viewpoint, Matt. He loves the old ways, which is why he hates the railroad. I did, too, until you pointed out that real towns would grow out of the debris of the dreadful boom-towns. Maybe Dad will see it some day. Deep in his heart he has a real admiration for Ty Whitman. And he did deliver beef to Whitman just as he had promised he would. Why, only last week he told me he'd deliver more if Whitman's price was right. Our whole crew is back in the hills now, cutting out stuff to build a herd for the railroad."

"Why not?" the Kid rasped. "The rustling of railroad beef is finished now that the hidden valley isn't any secret. A man couldn't *pretend* to be selling beef to the railroad any longer. He'd either have to actually deliver, or admit he'd as soon the graders starved."

Her eyes widened with horror. "I see," she said. "I see it all! You think Dad's a—a Judas! You think he's one of The Three!"

"God knows I don't want to think it!" The Kid's voice was dull with pain. "But I've got to go and talk to him, Lana, straighten this thing out—forever."

"No!" she cried and swung her horse to block the trail. "I can't let you! Can't you understand? He flayed you because he thought you were a sneaking dynamiter. He's sorry for that now, but you're still a railroad man. Dad would be bitter. You're bitter, too, and if you accused him of being one of The Three, he might say he was, just to spite you and Ty Whitman!"

"The blood call is strong, Lana."

"Dad clings to an idea like a burr clings to a saddle blanket," she hurried on. "He has the same opinion of you that I once had, the opinion we formed when we saw how Hank suffered for your sins. That's another reason I can't let you go to Dad. He doesn't know that the Gospel Kid is a different man than Matt McGrath of Texas. He liked Hank a lot, Matt. If you knew how much, you'd know that Dad couldn't be one of The Three."

* * *

Still the Kid's eyes were stern. The two were close to each other now and she laid a hand on his shoulder as she lifted her eyes to his.

"Matt," she said, "every girl meets a certain man some time—the *one* man. I always felt that I'd know mine the moment I saw him. Would it make any difference to you if I told you I met him beyond Crowfoot Gulch? Would it matter if I told you I wanted to hate him when I discovered who he was—but that I couldn't?"

He gently took her hand from his shoulder. "Would it matter?" he repeated. "Lana, I've always been a tumbleweed, and I never cared much if I ever took roots. Yet when I saw that hidden valley, I began thinkin' what a nice place it would be to have a spread with a few cattle under my iron. I've been lookin' for such a place ever since—since the night I stopped the train. Don't you savvy how it is with me, Lana? Can't you understand that I've been fighting against a showdown with Storm Herndon, fighting for two months now?"

In this most unorthodox fashion they declared their love and there was irony to transcend irony because what shone in her eyes was mirrored in the Kid's and yet he couldn't seal their declaration with a kiss, for there was still a lingering doubt in him.

"I want to believe you," he said hoarsely. "I—I do believe you. But why didn't you come and tell me the real reason he ran me off the place? Two months I've waited and wondered."

"I wanted to come," she said. "But I couldn't leave him again. You see, when he rolled down the gulch that night, he landed in a cluster of rocks. He was hurt, but he managed to reach his horse and get away. Since then he's grown steadily worse. The doctor from Deadman says he'll get over it in time. But for the last two months he's scarcely been able to leave a chair. There is no bitterness like the bitterness of a cripple, Matt."

"A cripple!" the Kid echoed, horror in his voice, and then he was remembering Storm Herndon half-rising from his chair and settling back again.

But he was thinking of something else, too, something that left him weak and trembling—a mental picture of himself forcing a showdown with a fiery, vitriolic rancher, Storm Herndon going for his gun and he, the Kid, beating him to the draw, only to discover too late that he'd fought a cripple!

"That's why I was repping for Dad with the herd," Lana went on. "I didn't tell you about it, because I knew you'd see for yourself when you met him."

"I'm mighty sorry, Lana," he said.

"I—"

That was as far as he got for suddenly guns were barking in the distance, echoing along the coulee. Those guns were speaking at the H-in-a-Hat ranchhouse, where a crippled oldster was, alone and defenseless. Instantly the man and the girl were spurring their horses in a wild gallop down the coulee which broadened out where the ranch buildings sprawled ahead of them.

Thundering away in the opposite direction, bent low over saddlehorns, were seven riders. Leading them was Cisco Yawberry, a bearded giant in a saddle. There was no mistaking him. But the Kid was more intent on following Lana who was hurling herself from her horse and running toward the long porch.

Then the Kid saw what she had seen, and the sight that met his eyes was proof enough that Storm Herndon was no ally of The Three. For Storm Herndon lay upon the planking of the porch in a shapeless heap, and his shirtfront was soggy with blood.

Quickly the Kid dropped to his knees beside the fallen rancher, making a brief but comprehensive examination. He glanced up, and he and Lana looked at each other across the body of her father. He read the desperate question in her agonized eyes.

"He's alive," he said.

She said nothing then, nor did she ever, to remind him that he had misjudged Storm Herndon.

"How badly is he hurt?" she asked, and drew a look of admiration from the Kid because her voice was so firm.

Along the Kid's smoky backtrail he had seen many men laid low by lead and he could gauge the seriousness of Herndon's wound with an accuracy that was almost professional.

"We've got to get him to a doctor as fast as we can take him there," he said. "I've fished out a few bullets in my time but I wouldn't dare probe for that one. It's too near his heart. Can you get a wagon ready?"

By the time she had a team hitched to a buckboard he had rummaged inside the house and found bandages, and whisky for an antiseptic, and had doctored the stricken rancher as best he could. Herndon's pulse was feeble but the thread of life was still there. The man and the girl lifted him into the wagon bed with infinite care, making the unconscious man as comfortable as possible in a nest of blankets. It was not until after they had put the ranchhouse behind them that Lana spoke again.

"They must have learned that Dad was going to keep on supplying the M.P. with beef!" she burst out. "That Yawberry outlaw was sent here to kill him if there was no other way to stop him!"

"But he isn't dead," the Kid reminded her. "And the doc out at end o' steel is a mighty good one. He'll patch him up pronto."

After that little was said. Lana, back in the wagon bed, crouched beside the still figure of her father. It was a nightmare journey, though, for contrition rode with the Gospel Kid. But with the realization that he had passed judgment on an innocent man came a determination to save the life of Storm Herndon if human endeavor could make that miracle possible.

It seemed an endless trek along an endless trail. His urge was to lash the team into a gallop, but on this rough ground he didn't dare. He could only crawl along, seemingly at a snail's pace, conscious that the slightest jar might lessen Herndon's chance of living.

Once the rancher opened his eyes. "You ain't tellin' me who I can sell my beef to," he muttered, and lapsed into unconsciousness again.

Obviously he was deliriously repeating something he'd said to Cisco Yawberry when that rustler and his crew had swooped down upon the ranch, evidence enough that Lana's intuition had been right, that she had unerringly put her finger on the reason for the shooting of her father.

The Kid's eyes were peeled for Yawberry and his riders as they rolled along. But the prairie lay bare before them as far as they could see. The long day spent itself at last, and darkness overtook them, but still they plodded onward.

• Chapter 14 •

Now at least there was a moon to light the way and the Gospel Kid, guided by Lana Herndon who knew this range, finally came onto a road of sorts. After that the wounded man was not jostled as badly as he had been. With the moon climbing above them and the stars sparkling against the dark canopy of the heavens, they headed toward end o' steel. And sometime during the night they reached the rails.

To Deadman town now, or to end o' steel? The Kid made a quick decision.

"End o' steel is closer and chances are the sawbones will be there," he said. "If he isn't, we can pack your dad back to town by train."

Lana smiled wanly. "We'll have to keep him unconscious if we expect to get *him* on a train, I imagine."

The Kid turned the team paralleling the rails. He watched for the headlight beams of a locomotive, hoping that a work train might come along. If one did, he could flag it and get Storm Herndon into camp far faster than in this slow-moving buckboard.

But the moon had faded by the time they reached the railroad tunnel and with it faded the Kid's hope that a train was running.

He knew there wasn't room enough for a wagon to skirt the tracks inside the bore, so had to force the team up onto the tracks, which shook the wagon violently. Lana cradled her father's head in her lap, easing some of the shock, and then they were in the black depth of the tunnel, guided only by the rails they followed. As fervently as the Kid had wished for the coming of a train before, he now prayed that the track would be clear. When they reached the end of the tunnel safely he sighed his relief.

"Four—five miles to camp," he told Lana.

Dawn was breaking as they came to the end of the steel. But the flame of life still flickered in Storm Herndon and the grueling race with death was nearly won.

They rounded a curve to see the camp sprawled ahead. Then the Kid knew instantly that something here was almighty wrong.

Men were swarming everywhere, pouring from tents and construction shacks in various stages of undress, rushing about like leaderless ants. Someone pounded an iron triangle. On a siding a locomotive puffed, its whistle beginning to scream.

Tyler Whitman was in the midst of it all, bareheaded, his gray hair flying as he gesticulated, issuing orders that were lost in the roar of startled voices. Leaping from the wagon seat, the Kid stumbled stiffly to him.

"What's goin' on?" he demanded.

"You're back!" Whitman roared. "Good! It's a showdown! Central Western has struck—hard. I should have expected something like this! We've got them licked so they've become desperate. They're risking everything to break our back with one blow!"

"But where are they striking?" the Kid asked.

"In Deadman. All night long Bottsinger's stage-coaches and freight wagons have been bringing men into town—toughs from the C.W. camps. They're taking over Deadman, lock, stock and barrel. They can tear up our tracks, keep supplies from coming through. And without steel we're bogged down—licked!"

"Storm Herndon's in that wagon," the Kid reported with a jerk of his thumb. "He was shot down, wounded bad, because he insisted on selling beef to you. Where's the doc?"

"Storm—wounded!" Whitman groaned. "The doctor went into Deadman with Kurt Ormond before the trouble broke. Key O'Dade started a message through when the toughs began taking over the town. Either the wire was cut or Key was dragged away from the instrument. The line's dead. But I'm taking every man into Deadman to give them their fight! I'll hook on my own coach. Have Storm loaded into it. We'll get him to the doctor!"

"Mister, I'm working for the railroad again," the Kid said, and was off.

Confusion was thrice multiplied as a locomotive backed up to a string of flat cars with Tyler Whitman's private car coupled to the front of them. Onto the flat-cars piled the M.P. workers, hundreds of them, and even horses were forced up plank inclines to be taken along. There were few guns in the camp but those available were passed around. The rest of the men chose hickory pickhandles, or any other sort of weapon they could lay their hands on.

Whitman personally supervised the loading of Storm Herndon into his car and climbed in. The Gospel Kid had one last glimpse of Lana's pale, strained face as she followed her father. Then the Kid swung into the locomotive cab just as the huge iron monster lurched to life, gathering momentum as it rolled along the unballasted roadway.

They were on their way to Deadman, the whole fighting force of the Montana-Pacific, to meet the challenge of the Central Western. Would they be too late to prevent the vandalism that would spell the finish of the M.P.? It was a desperate play the rival railroad was making, but if the Central Western was victorious today, then the Central Western would be victorious in the race for Government subsidization.

Let the matter come to court later. How could a bankrupt Montana-Pacific wage a courtroom battle? The real fight would be in Deadman.

There was Shadow Loomis to be considered but even though Loomis might report his findings to his superiors later, by his own admission he could identify only two of the three men who were behind this underhanded fight against the M.P. And Shadow Loomis might not even be alive.

The Kid's head was craned from the cab window while a sweating fireman toiled beside him. They were almost at the tunnel when the Kid suddenly saw Shadow Loomis ahead of them, in the middle of the track. He had emerged from the tunnel's black mouth astride a horse and he was racing straight toward the oncoming train, gesticulating wildly.

The engineer, leaning from the opposite window, saw the Government man, and reached for the brake lever. With steel grinding against steel as the train slid to a stop, the Kid was out of the cab just as Loomis flung himself from his horse.

"Thank God you stopped in time!" the man panted. "The tunnel's doomed!"

"Doomed!" the Kid echoed.

"It's going to be dynamited! I took to the hills like I told you I would. Not more than half an hour ago I saw riders working with dynamite, tamping charges into drill holes above the eastern end of the tunnel. The head of the outfit was that bearded fellow who's been around

Deadman a time or two lately—Yawberry, they call him. They're going to close the tunnel, I tell you!''

So shooting Storm Herndon wasn't the only devil's work that Cisco Yawberry had had to do for The Three! But that wasn't what made the Kid stare, horror and despair in his eyes. The tunnel was doomed! A thousand tons of rocks and earth would soon be blocking it, making it impassable for weeks. Truly The Three had planned a master stroke to defeat the M.P., for the fighting forces of the Montana-Pacific would be shut off from Deadman. They might reach the town by other routes, afoot and on horseback, but too late. And Storm Herndon who was dying would never reach the doctor in time!

''How soon will they be lighting the fuse?'' the Kid demanded. ''Quick! How much time is there left?''

''I don't know,'' Loomis said shakily. ''My idea was to get away and stop any train that might be coming. Maybe the fuse has already been lighted. Man, you aren't thinking of—''

But the Kid had swung back into the cab.

''I could pass the word back along the flatcars and take a vote,'' he said. ''That would take time we maybe haven't got to spare. I know these M.P. men, Loomis. I've worked with them for weeks and I know the way they'd want to do this. You with me, engineer? *We're going through that tunnel!*''

The engineer nodded, tightlipped. ''If this train goes any place, I go with it,'' he said and tugged at the throttle.

Shadow Loomis, something of both admiration and awe in his face, swung into the cab. Right behind him came Whitman who had clambered from his own car to learn the cause of the stop.

''I had to make the decision for you,'' the Kid said.

''But Herndon's girl!'' Whitman exclaimed. ''She's aboard, too!''

He didn't need to remind the Kid. But he thought of

the brave tilt of Lana's chin as she had asked how badly her father was wounded, her stoical suffering on the long ride across the prairie. The life of Storm Herndon depended on his getting into Deadman. The Kid made Lana's decision for her, knowing well what that decision would have been.

"She'd want it this way," he said softly.

The drivers spun and caught, and the train moved forward, picking up speed as it went. The dark mouth of the tunnel yawned and they were swallowed by it and only the glow of the firebox broke the enveloping darkness. A hush fell upon the four men in the cab, for the same thought was in the mind of each.

How many seconds before the mountain came down on top of them?

To the Kid it seemed as though the train crept at a snail's pace through the tunnel, but that was only because time was standing still. Actually the locomotive had gathered speed and in spite of the drag of the heavy load behind, it was running the tunnel faster than it had ever been run before.

With his head poked out of the cab window, the Kid saw the white eye of the tunnel's end through the choking, blinding smoke that bannered backward into his face. How far away that early daylight seemed!

Every sound was magnified—the scream of steam from the pistons, the pound of drivers over the unleveled rails, even the scrape of the fireman's shovel as he heaved coal into the firebox in a frenzy. Yet above all this bedlam, the Kid's ears were alert for the crack of doom, the first faint sound that might herald a devastating blast.

He heard it, too. But not until the locomotive had hurtled into the feeble dawn light again, and not until the last loaded flatcar was in the clear! Then the explosion came, the roar shaking the locomotive while the face of the mountain writhed before the Kid's horrified eyes. The wall above the tunnel groaned and collapsed. Then there was only billowing dust, the roar of a dynamite-sired avalanche, and the tunnel was sealed behind them.

"Stop the train!" Tyler Whitman ordered and the Kid wondered if his own face was as white and strained as the railroad builder's.

When the locomotive squealed to a stop again, Whitman piled out of the cab, but he returned shortly.

"Get going," he said briefly to the engineer, then turned to the Kid. "I unloaded a dozen men with guns and horses. Those dynamiters aren't far away and the boys have orders to round them up if it takes until Doomsday. The rest of us will clean up Deadman!"

• Chapter 15 •

Right after Whitman had his say the locomotive was moving again, and this time the heart of the iron cayuse might really have been in the race. With flanges screaming as they struck curve after curve, the cab swaying and pitching, it raced down the track toward Deadman, the engineer throwing his weight upon the whistle cord while the Kid spelled the weary fireman. And in this, Montana-Pacific's darkest hour, Matt McGrath sensed just how much the road had come to mean to him.

"I'm glad I got back in time," he told Whitman as Loomis took the shovel.

"Every fighting man will count, son," Whitman said. "I'm glad you finished your other business, too."

The Kid told him about it then, told him of his suspicion concerning Storm Herndon, and of the way he had been proved wrong. Whitman heard him in stupefied silence.

"If only you'd told me this in the first place!" the

railroad builder said. "I know Storm Herndon—better, perhaps, then he knows himself. He'd fight my road but he wouldn't fight me, any more than he would have fought Hank. We were his friends—Hank especially."

"I knew that." said the Kid. "But—"

"Storm Herndon knew Hank better than any man did." Whitman went on. "When we planned to send Hank's Bible to you, I told Kurt Ormond to check up with Storm Herndon before he got the package off to you. I told Kurt that if Hank had mentioned your address to any man, it was likely to have been to old Storm and—"

"Wait!" the Kid interjected. "Are you saying Kurt Ormond had Hank's Bible, that he sent it to me?"

"I wrote the letter the day of Hank's funeral," Whitman explained. "I stayed for the service but I was overdue back at division headquarters and had to leave Caprock. Kurt handled the details for me."

"I see," the Kid said slowly, and then Deadman was sprawling before them and the locomotive wheezed to a stop, its fighting freight unloading to swarm forward.

Up ahead, the narrow street was clogged with men—the C.W. toughs who had been brought in by The Three to take over the town. They were pouring toward the tracks, a surly, shouting mob, and the M.P. men met the challenge by charging to meet them. Wild war cries welled above the pounding of boots as the two factions crashed together—and the battle was on.

The Kid managed to restrain six of the M.P. men and sent them hurrying away in six different directions. Then he climbed into Whitman's private coach where Storm Herndon lay silent and gray-faced but still breathing.

"Six men have gone to look for the sawbones," the Kid explained to Lana. "They all know him and he'll be here pronto."

He moved toward the door but Lana caught his arm.

"And you, Matt?" she asked.

"I've got somebody else to look for," he said. "The Three are here, Lana."

"Be careful, Matt!" she whispered. "For my sake, be careful."

He kissed her then, holding her close. It was their first kiss and the thought shadowed the Kid that it might be their last. This was August second, wasn't it? Reluctantly he pulled himself away and swung out of the car without a word.

Chaos ruled in the street stretching ahead of him, a savage confusion of fighting men milling to make a sea of waving pickhandles while guns popped here and there. The Kid shouldered into the thick of it, his left fist lashing out, his right arm arcing as he laid his gun barrel across head after head, seeing men drop before him, seeing others take their places.

He caught a glimpse of Tyler Whitman, gray hair flying, and saw that soldierly oldster fighting hand to hand with a burly tough. And he saw Shadow Loomis lay that same tough low as the fellow pressed Whitman too hard.

It was tooth and toenail, first and club and gun and boot. It was Hades unleashed, men slugging and wrestling along the entire length of the street. Yet the Montana-Pacific men were fighting with the greatest fury, throwing their hearts and souls as well as their battered bodies into the conflict as though this had become a personal affair, which indeed it had. The Montana-Pacific men were remembering that dynamited tunnel and the fate that would have been theirs if the blast had gone off a minute or two sooner. Montana-Pacific was out for vengeance.

A club caught the Kid along the side of his head. He escaped the full force of the blow, for he saw it coming and twisted aside. But he lost his footing and went down, his head ringing, and was swept beneath a wave of slashing legs and trampling boots. He managed to get to his feet again and saw the red thatch of Key O'Dade in the press of men ahead of him and thrilled to the sight. He had feared that the telegrapher might have paid with his life for trying to get a message through to warn the end o' steel camp of the raid.

But O'Dade was here, fighting as savagely as any of the others, throwing himself into the conflict with a Celt's natural aptitude for such. There were others the Kid recognized, men he had worked with when the steel had pushed from Caprock to Lazura and Deadman and beyond. But the Kid did not see Durham or Bottsinger or the third man he sought.

He squeezed through the writhing wall of bodies and into the doorway of the Golden Slipper. The saloon was Durham's stronghold and the logical place to look for the man since Durham wasn't in the fighting. Inside the Golden Slipper, the Kid sagged against the wall, panting while he waited for his head to clear. The place was absolutely deserted.

He hadn't been in the Golden Slipper since it had moved to Deadman for Whitman's decree had barred all the M.P. men from the place. Besides the Kid had kept away from Durham when he had suspected Storm Herndon of being one of The Three. He had heard that Durham's business had suffered because of Whitman's blacklisting the saloon, and most of the percentage girls had deserted for more lucrative pleasure places. But the Kid had hardly expected to find the Golden Slipper completely empty.

Yet it was. The shelves were only half-stocked and there were plenty of empty bottles about, proof that the Central Western toughs had roistered here, fortifying themselves with liquor before they went about the devil's work they had come to do.

The roar of the fight in the street as the sound of the tumult beat through the thin walls accentuated the silence. The Kid crossed toward the bar, his boot heels thundering in the shrouding hush of the room.

When he felt unseen eyes upon himself he spun about, gun in hand, his own eyes probing every shadowy corner. For suddenly the feeling was strong upon him that he was in greater danger here than he had been in the street where death was rampant and disaster had a hundred forms. He tried to shake that feeling away, but it persisted. Yet where was the danger in this deserted place?

He approached the bar, wondering if he'd find a barkeep cowering behind the long counter. His eyes flicked to the full-length mirror behind the bar and, like that other time when he had walked into the Golden Slipper in Caprock, he saw the reflections of the oil paintings on the wall behind him, especially "The Lady of the Nile.' And, unbelievably, just for a second the picture again had the semblance of life.

But this time the Kid understood—and realized his danger. Shadow Loomis had been in Hoyt Durham's office once. Shadow Loomis knew the secret of that trick picture. Loomis had spoken of it to the Kid in Caprock, warning the Kid in a way, though the Kid had failed to understand at the time.

"A pretty picture, eh?" the man had said. "She can see, friend, and she can hear. And some day she'll speak."

It had sounded idiotic at the time. But "The Lady of the Nile" was speaking now, speaking with a fiery tongue that blazed from her face. For gunflame was lashing through the picture, straight at the Gospel Kid!

He felt the burn of the bullet as it bored into his thigh, spinning him about and slamming him against the bar. His knees caved and he fell to the floor, fighting against the darkness that threatened to claim him. He lay there like a dead man.

There had to be a room somewhere above. The Kid could see flimsy stairs in one shadowy corner, leading to the second floor. Slowly he tottered toward the stairs, wondering if his strength would sustain him until he reached them. . . .

Hoyt Durham's private office in Deadman's Golden Slipper was much like his office in Lazura and in Caprock had been—another ornately furnished room built below the floor level of the second story. In this latest windowless sanctuary, Durham came to his feet, letting the leather flap on the wall fall into place.

"Got him!" he announced, his swarthy face triumphant. "That idea you had of shooting through the picture made it a cinch, Curly. Matt McGrath is stretched out on the floor—dead!"

Curly Bottsinger grinned. "Reckon we'd better tote his carcass out, eh?" he suggested.

The third man shook his head. "No hurry," he argued. "There'll be plenty of dead men in this town before the sun goes down. And nobody to ask questions about them. We'll be the winners, and the winners don't have to answer to anybody."

"But what about this Loomis galoot?" Bottsinger said worriedly. "Suppose he's snooping for the Government, like you figured he might be? Suppose he reports this raid and the C.W. has to answer for it?"

The third man eased his gun from its holster, spun the cylinder calculatingly and replaced the weapon.

"We gave Loomis until the fifteenth to run or take the consequences," he remarked reflectively. "But now, with matters going as they are, we won't wait that long. No use leaving any loose ends. I didn't see Loomis around last night but he's probably still in town. Who's to say what happened if he stops a bullet during the street fighting? If there's a Government investigation on account of him, we'll claim the M.P. started the fracas when we brought men into town for our own protection. We'll say Loomis got cut down during the fight. Right now one of us had better get outside and find him."

"That'll be pretty risky," Durham observed. "Let's cut for low card to see who does the job."

He bustled about the room in search of a deck of cards, finding one in a commodious drawer of his desk after a lengthy search. Breaking the seal, he shuffled the pasteboards, his jeweled fingers winking in the lamp light as he fanned out the cards, face down, on the table top. Each man selected a card, the third man smiling as he faced his—the deuce of clubs.

"That's about the way it should be," Durham decided. "We're starting around the circle again. I burned down Matt McGrath. Curly here got Dan Callishaw. And you're the gent who pumped a bullet into Hellvation Hank. Now it's your turn again. You—"

"Reckon not," said the Gospel Kid, standing framed in the open doorway, a bloody, disheveled figure. But the gun in his hand was steady. "Raise 'em" he ordered. "Careful, Ormond! You'll never get that gun out of leather!"

• Chapter 16 •

Kurt Ormond stood stock-still. His lips twisted a little as he looked at the Gospel Kid.

"So now you know," he said evenly.

"Now I know you're the one who got Hank," the Kid said. "I heard Durham put the deadwood on you just as I stood outside the door. But I'm not surprised to find that you're one of the The Three, Ormond, you already gave yourself away."

"I don't think so," Ormond scoffed. "The man who made a slip was Hoyt when he thought you were dead, just because you fell."

"You slipped too, Ormond," the Kid said in a deadly tone. "You slipped when you had that headboard left in my tent—with my birth date on it. I couldn't think how anybody hereabouts knew my birth date until Whitman told me you'd had Hank's Bible last fall. *My birth date was on the family record page!* Did you figure, even last fall, Ormond, that knowing my birth date might come in handy sometime?"

Ormond laughed. "January first was easy to remember. Somehow the year stuck in my mind, too. When we made up that headboard I thought it would be more impressive with your birth date. I never guessed you'd be able to figure out where the information came from. For other gents we had Thackery Weaver's list. We borrowed his files."

"I know," said the Kid. "Was a time when I thought Weaver might be one of The Three. I know now you're Judas all right—a sneaking double-crosser who pretended to work for the Montana-Pacific when you've been on the Central Western's payroll all along. And you're a sight worse than the first Judas, Ormond. He was decent enough to string himself up."

"Judas?" Ormond repeated. "You mean—"

"I mean I've been looking for three gents like Goliath and Herod and Judas. Hank left that much sign for me."

Ormond's eyes widened. "Those blood smears in Hank's Bible! I saw them, too! But I thought Hank had probably pawed the pages accidentally as he was dying."

The Kid realized that Ormond was stalling for time, but within the Kid was a great weariness and a desire to be done with this business.

"One of you is as guilty as another," he said with the solemnity of a judge pronouncing sentence. "It's been a long trail, and this is the end of it. But the devil of it is that I can't shoot you like I—"

Bottsinger stared at him incredulously. "You mean you ain't goin' to gun us down?"

"Not the way you think" the Kid said. "Not the way you'd do business, you back-shooting skunks! Was a time when I wouldn't even be wastin' words on you. You can thank Hellvation Hank for the chance you're going to get. I had to study his Bible to read the sign he'd left for me and, reading that Bible, I began to see that my way was the wrong way. That's what's made the difference between the Gospel Kid and Matt McGrath of Texas. But Hank was my brother and I can't forget that, either. ' "Vengeance is mine," sayeth the Lord'. But maybe I'm to be His instrument of vengeance today. But—you don't even savvy what I'm talkin' about!"

He slipped his gun into holster.

"Get at it," he said with a vast disgust.

Just for an instant he stood there weaponless, giving them the chance they hadn't given Hank McGrath or Dan Callishaw. Then, their first astonishment passing, they were doing exactly what the Kid had known they would do—going for their guns. Hoyt Durham was the first to unlimber his six-shooter and Durham was the first to die. The Kid's hand darted downward and came up with fire blossoming from it. He shot Durham just as the dandified saloon owner was earing back the hammer of his weapon.

But that instant had given Bottsinger and Ormond time to unleather their guns. Those guns spat, driving splinters from the door jamb on either side of the Kid. The Kid leaped into the room then, feeling the burn of a bullet along his shoulder, the bit of another as it nicked the lobe of his ear. But he was firing before his feet touched the floor and Bottsinger crumpled into a corner, a bullet-hole between his shaggy brows.

The Kid landed sprawling, for the excruciating pain that welled from his wounded thigh as he struck the floor made his legs turn rubbery. A bullet zipped over his head, another burned along his ribs.

Kurt Ormond was firing with the coolness that characterized him. Propping himself upon one elbow, the Kid sighted carefully. The gun belched and Ormond wilted before him.

"You—win," Ormond managed to say and the mask-like expression was gone from his inscrutable face. "You should—have been on—on our side—" He pitched face forward, dead.

Ormond's fingers clutched at the table as he fell, fastening upon the silk tablecloth. The lamp was overturned. Instantly burning kerosene was showering everywhere, lapping across the floor toward the flimsy walls as a sheet of flame leaped across the room.

Out of that inferno the Kid dragged himself to the hallway. With the wall to support him, he groped toward the flimsy stairs, with smoke billowing down the corridor, flames roaring behind him. The fire was spreading fast in this tinderbox building that was half tent and half structure and there were flames in the hallway before the Kid inched along to the stairs. Getting down he always remembered as a nightmare—hazy and horrible. But he made it. He reached the street just as part of the second story collapsed.

Men were still battling along the boardwalks and in the dusty road between them. But hostilities ceased temporarily as eyes turned toward the Golden Slipper where smoke billowed to hide the sky. In the sudden hush the Kid raised his voice.

"The Three are dead—inside!" he shouted. "Your paymasters won't be payin' off for C.W. tonight!"

Two or three swollen jaws sagged in surprise. A half dozen toughs took to their heels, shouting M.P. workers hard after them. Then Tyler Whitman was beside the Kid, leading him away from the doomed saloon.

"That finishes it," the railroad builder said. "The telegraph wasn't destroyed. Those fellows just dragged O'Dade away from the key when he tried to warn us this morning. Loomis wired to Fort Yellowstone. He's a Government man and his authority was enough to impress them. Soldiers are on the way here to declare martial law but I guess we won't need them. The toughs have already begun to run out."

"Then we've won!" the Kid babbled.

"Won?" Whitman echoed and he was just as white

and strained-looking as he had been when they had run that doomed tunnel.

"We've cleaned up Deadman," Whitman conceded. "But we've lost, son—lost! The Central Western will swear these toughs weren't on their payroll. The C.W. is far behind but they'll beat us now that the tunnel's down. It'll take weeks to clear it out and we're tied up until we do. We can't get a yard of steel out to the end of the line otherwise!"

Just for a second the Kid looked into the crestfallen face of this fighting railroad builder who had been his brother's friend, this man who had made the good fight against all the odds and who had fought on, even when defeat had seemingly already overtaken him. Then the Kid was laughing wildly, deliriously.

"A tunnel!" he shouted. "Mister, I'll hand you a tunnel all roped and saddled and ready to ride! A ready-made tunnel that can be put into shape to be a railroad tunnel in a tenth of the time it would take to clear out your tunnel. And it will be a more direct route, too. I would have told you all about it before but the M.P. tunnel was already dug and it didn't make much difference then. Besides, it was part of the story concerning Storm Herndon that I kept to myself. Ty, this tunnel's exactly what you want! Kurt Ormond must have known that when he looked over the country. But he was one of The Three, working against the M.P., not for it!"

Tyler Whitman regarded him queerly, doubt, astonishment and a great elation having their successive turns in the railroad builder's eyes.

"Things are coming a mite fast for me, boy," he said at last. "I'm hoping you're not out of your head. The doctor's busy. He's working on Storm Herndon. He says the old gent is going to pull through, too. We'd better march down there and have the doc look you over."

Whitman supported the Kid on the one side and Key O'Dade appeared to bolster Matt McGrath's faltering footsteps on the other. As they made their way toward the railroad tracks triumph walked with the Kid along the dusty street of Deadman for his work was nearly done. And if the pace was far too slow to suit his mood, it wasn't because a *doctor* was waiting in the coach.

Another April. The snow had come and gone again. In the upper reaches of the Big Thunders occasional white patches still lingered although the foothills had long since donned their mantles of green.

The Kid and Lana had taken all morning to climb to a promontory where they sat their saddles, looking down into the valley where twin rails glistened in the sunlight.

"I never see the railroad without remembering Dad's change of heart," she said. "And yet I always knew he was not as bitter as he pretended to be. He only needed an excuse to make his peace with Tyler Whitman. When Whitman's train got him to the doctor in time to save his life, he had his excuse."

"Seems like a mighty long time ago," the Kid remarked gravely. "The Three are dead. Cisco Yawberry and his outfit are in prison for that dynamiting job. And the Central Western has given up. The last time I saw Ty Whitman, he told me they'd sold their Montana holdings to him for a fraction of their worth. The northern track will be a spur of the Montana-Pacific."

"You never say much about those meetings with Tyler Whitman," Lana observed pointedly.

The Kid smiled. "He made me another offer," he admitted. "He can't get it through his head that I'd rather run a few dogies of my own than help run somebody else's railroad. But speaking of your dad, why hasn't he been to the valley lately?"

Lana laughed again. "He's practically letting the crew run the H-in-a-Hat and since he's well enough to get around again he's spending more and more time in

Deadman.'' she said. ''He and Key O'Dade have struck up quite a friendship. Dad's becoming a dyed-in-the-wool railroad man. It's terrible the way those two have contaminated each other. Number Twenty-seven was ten minutes late as usual and Dad was fuming. 'Faith and it's a fine way to be runnin' a railroad!'' he said. And what do you suppose O'Dade had to say to that? 'I reckon you're plumb right,' he agreed. 'I'll pile onto the telegraph and see if I can dab a loop on that maverick!' ''

The Kid joined in her laughter but his eyes were thoughtful as the sweep of his hand took in the valley with the steel stretching from east to west.

''It's finished,'' he said. ''And it's already bringing a new day to the range. Look at how Caprock and Lazura and Deadman are building a real prosperity on the ruins of their boom-towns. There's Hellvation Hank's monument, Lana—the railroad. It makes me proud to think I had a hand in the building of it.''

She looked at him long and tenderly and the laughter was gone from her.

''You think *that* is what you built that would make Hank the proudest?'' she asked softly.

''What better?'' he countered.

''Have you seen the latest edition of Thackery Weaver's paper? He's clamoring for folks to build a church mighty soon. He says that now that we have another fighting sky-pilot on the range, it isn't seemly for folks to be crowding into his little ranchhouse in Hidden Valley in order to hear him read from Hank McGrath's Bible. You've built a new life for yourself, Matt. I think that's the thing Hank would like.''

The Kid grinned his easy grin. ''Shucks, I had to make a few changes, didn't I?'' he argued. ''Wasn't no other way to convince your dad that his girl wasn't throwin' herself away on a worthless, wide-loopin', hell-bent gun-boss!''

They were close to each other and his arms went

around her. And the Gospel Kid, that tumbleweed who had at last taken roots, kissed his bride and had his kiss returned. Somewhere in the distance a locomotive's whistle wailed. The valley walls caught the mournful sound, toying with it until even the echoes finally faded into the thin silence of the high country.

GUN-RIDER

• Chapter 1 •
Last Chip

CURLY MATHER FETCHED THE NEWS TO HIS BOSS, coming into the hotel dining room with his spurs jangling, crossing with an intent directness of purpose to the table where Dan Saxon took his supper with his daughter Rita. Mather stood tall beside the table, a hard-muscled, weather-burned, youngish man with no laughter in him. "Well," he announced, "he's here. Want to come and take a look at him?"

Saxon smiled. "Don't you suppose I heard the stage roll in?"

Mather said sourly, "I figgered you'd be interested."

Saxon toed out a chair. "Sit down, Curly, and have a piece of pie. Perhaps it will be the last one Circle-S will ever buy you. Why should I care that Long Tom Randall's got to town? Telford's finished me off already. Randall won't even have to earn his pay."

He said this so calmly that Mather looked quickly at Rita Saxon as if seeking confirmation from her, Mather's eyes asking, *Is it so?* Rita had a sultry sadness to her tonight; she was a vibrant girl, olive-skinned and sloe-eyed as her Spanish mother had been; and she had the same liquid grace to her movements and the same promise of passion in her full lips. Mather looked at her and was at once hungry for her, forgetting everything else.

Dan Saxon, seeing this, said with faint irony, "She's the daughter of a busted rancher, Curly. Telford has picked up my notes from the bank. I learned that today. I got a wagonload of grub from Barney Shay, but he told me the mercantile would have to see cash on the barrel head from here on out. What is there left for this Tom Randall to do?"

Mather said harshly, "Then you've given up fighting?"

Saxon looked at him, seeing the recklessness in Mather's solid features, seeing the impatience, and Saxon sighed for years gone and youth lost. "No," he said. "There is one last fling in me—one more chip to be spent. I'll have a look at this Long Tom Randall."

He stood up from the table and was, as always, a living contradiction, a man with saddle swagger to his walk and the stamp of Montana's wind and rain and sun upon his long, aristocratic face; yet he favored a knee-length plantation-style coat and a string tie, and he had hands that were long and tapering—gambler's hands. Something about him spoke of vast acres and cattle bred with meticulous care. Something about him flung you back thirty years to Mississippi gambling boats and Mississippi showboats. This anachronism was Dan Saxon. He looked like a man with no more on his mind than an evening at cards or a few hours with old cronies discussing feed and the price of beef.

But Rita cried out suddenly, "Dad—!"

Saxon's thought then was that she knew him—she knew him full well—and from her knowledge came her fear. He was a softened man then. He had raised her to face fear, to face all the realities; but at this particular moment he wanted to spare her, so he said, "I plan only to do whatever needs to be done, Rita. I'll be back in a few minutes."

He crossed the clattersome dining room to the lobby, leaving Rita with Curly Mather at the table. He made it a point to pause at the cashier's desk and buy a cigar, letting Rita see him do this. A few of the stage passengers were already filtering into the hotel; and once into the lobby, Saxon elbowed among these, past the chairs where loiterers sat with their newspapers and their eternal idleness.

One of these men looked up at him and said, "Good evening, Dan."

Saxon said, "Good evening, Gault."

Gault Telford was a man running to flesh, a moon-faced man whose face looked oddly proportioned, for thick lenses enlarged his eyes, making them big and startling. Telford said mildly, "Are you of a mind to sell now, Dan?"

Saxon gave him a soft smile and said, "And what would that add up to for me, once my notes were paid off?"

"A few thousand, Dan. I am not a haggling man. Nor am I a spiteful one. I don't wish to push you to the wall. Come around tomorrow and talk about it. You need never have to fight a Montana winter again. There is St. Louis or San Antone, or wherever your fancy may take you. A gentleman's cloth for you, Dan, a lady's life for your girl."

Saxon very carefully stowed away the unlighted cigar. "And all Sleeping Cat Basin one big syndicate of ranches with Gault Telford at their head."

"With you as my right hand, if you'd rather stay in Montana," Telford said. "We have known each other many years, my friend. Let's not have the ambition of either of us lay a shadow on our friendship."

Dan Saxon smiled. "They tell me Long Tom Randall just climbed off the stage."

Something showed in Telford's magnified eyes, something feral that was at once gone. "Sleeping Cat has become a tough town, Dan, with that railroad spur driving deeper into the hills every day. Count noses on the street and see how many construction crew men are here spending their pay. It's my town, and I want it an orderly town. That's why I sent for Long Tom. You're jumping at shadows, Dan."

Saxon said, "Ah, yes. And for a solid month every bartender and hostler and roustabout has been telling me that Randall was coming. And naming the day and the hour. Why was that?"

"When a man is a legend, Dan, people talk about him."

Saxon said, "I'll go see how broad this one is."

He walked out upon the hotel's gallery and stood there at the head of the three steps leading down to the boardwalk. Diagonally across the way stood the stage station, logs silvered by weather. The Concord had now gone; and the crowd, drawn always by the excitement of its coming, had dispersed; and there was no man to be seen who held Dan Saxon's interest.

Sleeping Cat lay around him, two straggly rows of false fronts facing across a river of dust, a town born of cattle, a town born of chaos. The hitch racks were full, and at this hour the lamps were just beginning to blossom. Cowboys rode in from the far reaches of the basin; the hills hemming the basin were yonder shapes, vague in the dusk. Cowboys jangled their spurs along the boardwalks, but the planking gave back also the echo of the boots of railroad construction workers, a new breed on the land. Sleeping Cat's population had taken to tripling with each sundown. Dan Saxon stood looking at Sleeping Cat, and he said, softly, "You're an ugly old town."

Then Long Tom Randall shaped up in the doorway of the stage office across the street.

He looked like a man hard-driven by the winds of chance, a man at once wolf-wary and wolf-wise. There was dignity to him, the proud bearing of one who had carved out his name in that Johnson County affair and had sent his name before him and had now to walk erect in the shadow of it. He was young—Saxon pegged him at about twenty-five—but he was also old, old as the hills, old as violence, old as Cain. He wore range garb and carried a single gun belted low; his hat was flat-brimmed and slanted above a face that was gaunt and saturnine. He was Long Tom Randall, imported gunman. And he was walking across the street toward the hotel where Dan Saxon stood.

There was only a brief span of waiting, and yet it was long enough to send Saxon's memory rushing back across all the years—the riverboat years, and the war years, and the mavericking in Texas, and the long trail north; the good years and the bad years; the accumulated years that had brought him to this night and this moment. He wondered then if all of his living had been fashioned for this, if each turn of the trail had been meant to direct his footsteps to a given place and a given time. He wondered, and knew a certain target, and a certain glory.

And then, strangely, looking at Long Tom Randall, he saw himself as he had been before those years had burdened him, young and lithe and proud, a hundred chips to be played and all of life a game. Then he shrugged and came down to the boardwalk and moved a few paces along it until he was directly in line with Randall. Raising his voice, he said, "That's just about far enough, friend."

Long Tom Randall stopped in the dust of midstreet, brought up short by the challenge. When he lifted his head, his nostrils flared in the manner of a fighting man; he was at once smelling trouble and readying himself for it. His eyes measured Saxon, and he said, "I don't recollect knowing you."

"I'm the man you were fetched here to kill," Saxon said.

"Ah," Long Tom said and drew in a hard, full breath.

* * *

Saxon became conscious then of every small sound of the town, the distant voice of the summer wind in the cottonwoods, the clamor from the hotel, the stomping of a horse at a nearby hitchrail. He knew that men had paused in their striding, seeing here the shape of trouble and watching it out. He brushed back the skirt of his long coat and exposed his gun, hooking a thumb close to it. "It might as well be here and now," he said.

Long Tom shook his head, not believing this. "You're a damn' fool."

"No, Randall. Just a man with one chip left."

Randall said, "I've got no fight with you. Not yet."

Saxon said, "Must I find the words to make you fight? Is that it? Do you always have to pick the time and the place yourself? Maybe you want a high cutbank and your man on the road below you."

Randall took a spreadlegged stand, his shoulders hunched slightly forward. "Start it!" he said.

Saxon made his move, his eyes holding tight on Randall, and in him afterwards was no true remembrance of how the rest came about. He knew that he got his own gun out of leather; he felt its weight in his hand and had a surety in that moment that he had bested Randall by the split-second that made all the difference. Then gun-thunder was in his ears, reverberating from the false fronts and filling the dusk, and pain was everywhere, running up from his hand and through him. His gun lay fallen in the dust at the boardwalk's edge. Randall stood with his own gun poised, smoke curling from it and lifting to the breeze and floating away.

Saxon looked down at his right hand and saw that a long furrow had been raked across the back of it.

Randall came toward him and paused. He gave Saxon a look, revealing nothing, neither compassion nor anger; but he said, "I could have shattered your wrist as easy. I hope you've got out of your craw whatever you had in it, mister."

Rita was there suddenly, come running out of the hotel, the high stand of Curly Mather looming behind her. Rita cried, "Dad—!" her voice both scared and angry. Long Tom Randall looked at her and lifted his hat and went on. Dan Saxon got a handkerchief from the breast pocket of his coat. "You'll have to help me, girl," he said.

She wrapped the handkerchief around his bleeding hand. "We'll get you down to Doc Farrell's."

She commenced leading him along the boardwalk, Mather hurrying to flank them, looking sour and troubled. To his foreman Saxon said, "Go get the wagon hooked up and ride out with it. I'm staying in town tonight."

Mather said angrily, "Are you hellbent on getting yourself killed?"

Saxon said, "Do as I say!" He watched Mather go angling across the street, walking stiffly. He said then, "He hasn't married Circle-S, not yet!"

Rita said, "Randall had forty years the best of you. Did you go crazy?"

"No," Saxon said. "I knew the edge was his. I tried to offset those years by choosing him when he was stiff from travel, and hungry, perhaps, and tired, and not yet expecting trouble. It was all the advantage I could get, and it might never come again."

Rita said, "You forced it on him! And what did you gain by it?"

"Why," Saxon said, "I took his measure. He's whang-leather all the way through, and he'll chew cactus and spit out the spikes. But he's got a soft spot. Don't you see? He could have killed me, but he was content to shoot the gun out of my hand and let it go at that. He opened himself up like a book and let me read him."

They were beyond the business establishments of the street and nearing a cottage surrounded by a white picket fence. At its gate, Rita took her hand from her father's arm. "Now go in and tell Doc Farrell that you've just been the biggest damned fool on Sleeping Cat range."

She turned away, and he asked, "Where are you going?"

"To Rube's barber shop to borrow a pair of shears," she called back. "All your way got you was a bloody hand. I'm going to play Delilah to this Samson. Could you use another rider if I hired one?"

Long Tom Randall came into the hotel and crossed its lobby to the desk, men making room for him and the talk of men falling to a faint buzz. This was not to his liking, this having been spotlighted by that incident on the street; and he felt edgy and was weary of people and the ways of people. There were times when he envied the small, obscure ones who did the small, obscure tasks of the world. This was one of those times.

The desk clerk, a pimpled youth, said, "Mr. Randall? We have a room ready for you."

Randall said, "My warsack is over at the stage depot," and put his signature down and pocketed the extended key and climbed a carpeted stairs to the hall above. His room faced on the street and was a good one as cowtown hotel rooms went. This was not the Cheyenne Club, but it was the best Sleeping Cat had to offer.

The door closed behind him; he looked at the bed and bureau, then moved to the window and looked down upon Sleeping Cat. Presently there came a knock. Randall was at once wary, but it was the pimpled clerk fetching his warsack. When the boy had gone, Randall probed into his fixings and got a clean shirt and stripped to the waist and gave himself a washing. Then he shaved. He was wiping the last of the lather away when Gault Telford stepped into the room.

Randall came about quickly, crouched like a cat and moving sidewards to where he'd hung his gun belt on a bedpost, but Telford said, "Easy, friend. I'm the man you've been expecting."

Randall said, "Some day you're going to come through a door without knocking, mister, and they'll be dusting out the black wagon for you."

Amusement shone through Telford's thick lenses. Standing, he was a pear-shaped man, scrupulously neat, carefully tailored, a mild and inoffensive man to the eye. Randall had seen horses with that same quiet, half-asleep look to them. And he had been pitched into the dust when such horses had exploded beneath him.

Telford said, "I don't think you understand. I'm Gault Telford."

"Next time, you knock!"

Telford let himself down upon a chair. "I like a careful man. As of now, you're working for me."

"As of tomorrow, maybe. Tonight I want a steak an inch thick and a yard wide. And I want to take the stagecoach kinks out of me in that bed. You're a man who jumps to conclusions, mister. And by the way, that letter of yours was damn' sketchy."

Telford's serenity remained unruffled. He threw out an arm and made a vast circling motion. "This is my town and my range. Sometimes small dogs nip at my heels. Your job will be to kick them out of the way. Two hundred a month and cartridges. Did Wyoming pay you that well?"

Randall grinned, the grin making a great, grim slash across his face. "Then you owe me the first cartridge. I used it out on the street. Another thing your letter didn't say was that there'd be a reception committee."

"That was Dan Saxon, the only independent rancher left in the basin. If you'd finished him then and there, I'd be shelling out a bonus right now."

"That wasn't in the letter, either," Randall said.

Telford leaned forward. "Look, friend, you're proddy. Saxon did the unexpected, and that made a surprise for me and a bad moment for you. You got started on the wrong foot tonight, so you're showing me your teeth. I'm not here to play a game with words.

There is one chunk of ground in this basin that is not yet mine—Saxon's Circle-S. I've got him nearly to the wall. Money is the sinews of war, and I've just about broke him. I've brought you in to finish the job. Do you want the work?"

"I don't operate from cutbanks in the dark of the moon."

"You won't have to. Saxon has got one last chance. He knows it and I know it. Prairie Pacific is building a railroad spur into the hills. The graders need beef, and Saxon has been angling for a contract to supply it. They will pay premium prices, and that cash could be the saving of Circle-S. I do not want his beef delivered to the grading camps. It is as simple as that."

Long Tom Randall said, "It could be interesting." He stood silent then, and thoughtful, a practical man weighing the odds in his mind. But he was also a fanciful man, liking in this proposition the challenge to his imagination and ingenuity. He stood in the gathering dusk, his naked torso gleaming whitely in odd contrast to his sunburned face. He said again, "It could be interesting."

"Then it's a deal," Telford said emphatically, and arose.

"Not yet," Randall said.

Telford frowned. "Why not?"

"You're a man who takes things for granted—including doors. You need a lesson in politeness, mister, and one in patience. Come around tomorrow morning and we'll talk again."

All the affability went out of Telford, but the metallic anger that rose in his eyes never quite reached his lips. He stood for a moment like some graven, glass-eyed Buddah, and then he said, "To a man like you, I would give a free rein on any job. I would ask no questions as long as the job were done. But I demand respect. Do you understand that?"

Randall grinned again. "The thing you're forgetting is that I'm not working for you yet. Come around tomorrow."

Telford put his hand to the doorknob. "I choose to think that your long trip has tired you and that what happened between you and Saxon was a further drain on your nerves. Because I choose to think that, I shall overlook your attitude."

Randall's grin broadened. "Good. That's as close to a deal as we need come just now. You choose to think what you damn' please, and I'll choose to think my way. Good-night, Mr. Telford."

After Telford had closed the door, Randall was of a mind to turn the key, but he didn't. He went again to the window and stared down upon Sleeping Cat. In him was a slow anger and an old rebellion. You put yourself up for hire, and the Gault Telfords sent for you, wanting not only your gun and your skill but every part of you, inside and out. You had your price, and your self-respect was supposed to be tossed into the bargain. He had met the Gault Telfords before, and the only difference in a pattern grown dull with repetition was one town and another. But even the towns got so they were the same.

With such thinking, his weariness became more than physical. And so he stood at the window and watched the night enfold Sleeping Cat while the lamps blossomed to yellow the dust.

At the tap on the door, he swung about, fretful and frowning, for he supposed that Telford had returned, and he was in no mood for Telford. He said, "Come in."

A girl opened the door and stood framed, and he at once remembered her as the one who'd come rushing to that man he'd shot, that Dan Saxon. He still hadn't donned his shirt, and he was suddenly conscious of this and made a move toward the fresh one he'd laid out on the bed.

The girl said, "I'm Rita Saxon."

He gave her a level look. "And you've come to tell me what you think of what happened on the street."

"No," she said, "I've come to say there are no hard feelings. Aren't you going to ask me in?"

He picked up the shirt and got into it and buttoned it after a fashion. He made a poor job of tucking the shirt into his pants. He lifted his gun belt from the bed post and swung it around his middle, then moved to the bureau and got the lamp lighted. Looking at Rita, he shrugged. "Come in, if you wish. What's on your mind?"

In the lamplight she was a mighty pretty girl with that soft olive skin and those eyes that took a man back to Texas and languid Rio nights. She moved into the room and closed the door and put her back to it and smiled at him, her smile warm and inviting. "I've been waiting. I knew you had company, but I saw him leave. Is it too late to ask you to change sides?"

Randall said, "You're fetching me an offer from Circle-S."

"Forty a month and found," she said. "Moving a bunch of cattle up into the hills. Long hours and hard ones. No pay till the job is done. It doesn't begin to meet Telford's offer, does it?"

He grimaced. "Not yet."

She came farther into the room; she had a liquid way of walking, a sinuous movement to her hips. She smiled at him again, and this time her smile was both an invitation and a challenge. "I'm sure," she said, "you'd find it pleasant working for Circle-S. I'll try to make it so."

Now he understood, and he threw back his head and laughed. His laughter boomed in the room. He saw her smile fade and chagrin draw down her lips, and she said, "Whatever is funny must only be funny to you."

He said, "I've seen hussies try to play the part of ladies. That was funny enough. But not nearly so funny as a lady trying to play a hussy."

She said with quick anger, "You needn't draw an inference! What I said implied no promise."

"Of course not," he said. "That's where the joke comes in. I'm to go to work for Circle-S. At the end of a day's work, if I'm not so dead beat out that I can't think of anything but my soogans, the boss' beautiful daughter will maybe go riding with me. When I try to kiss her, she'll tuck in her chin, but she'll do it with a laugh so I'll be fool enough to try another night. We'll play that kind of game till the work's done. Then I'll get my forty a month. And the boss' daughter will be mighty busy whenever I come around."

Color crept into her face, and he was sure she was going to slap him. Instead, she said, "You want your payment in advance, is that it?"

Her boldness caught him off balance; she was all femininity in the lamplight, a woman wholly desirable; yet there was about her a man's forthrightness that made him puzzled. He said soberly, "You're bluffing!"

She turned back toward the door. He thought she was going to slam through it angrily, but she turned the key and then faced about. She said in a small voice, "Circle-S has very little to offer. I see you want your bargains pat. You can name it now."

That was when he saw that she was scared—scared yet brave and determined. He stared at her, not believing what she implied, yet having to believe it; and in that moment he hated Gault Telford and hated himself and all his way of life. She stood there for the taking, and his blood thundered in his temples, but it was her very willingness that defeated him, for he could tell from what desperation her willingness was wrought.

He said in a softer voice, "I was born twenty years too late. Once a man could swing a wide loop in the Texas brush and build up a herd from the mavericks that belonged to ranchers scattered to hell-and-gone by the war. Anybody could become a cattle king overnight. I had to come along too late for that. For me and my kind it has to be forty bucks a month. But when I was old enough to think, I decided that I'd play for bigger stakes than that, or I wouldn't play at all. That's what fetched me from Texas to Wyoming. That's what fetched me here. Telford offered the biggest stake. That's all there is to it."

Rita said, "And where will that take you? From one gun job to another! Until some day you're the old man who stands in the street and faces a young man the way my father faced you today."

He said, "I'll have a ranch of my own before that day. I'm no fool who earns it fast and spends it fast. This town, this job, is just one rock in the crossing of a wide creek."

She shook her head; she had dropped all pretense of coquetry. "That's nothing but plain selfishness! I ought to feel sorry for you."

He said, "What's the difference between us? What I want, I go after in my own way. You have your way. It just happens that I don't want to buy your bargain."

She said, "Here's the difference: whatever I'd be willing to do is for somebody else—an old man who spent his last chip tonight."

"Sure," he said, "so it would be only half a bargain. That's not a game."

Her chin came up. "The Saxons gamble," she said, "but they never cheat!"

He walked toward her. He hooked his hands under her arms and lifted her from her feet. He swung her and got an arm under her knees, and he saw the fear naked in her eyes then, and he saw the courage. He crossed to the bed and tossed her there and turned and twisted the key in the door, unlocking it. He went out into the hall, leaving the door half open behind him, and started for the stairs.

Halfway down the stairs, he said, "Hell!" saying it aloud, saying it softly. Then he began laughing again and came into the lobby laughing. It struck him that the sour taste Gault Telford had left in his mouth had been washed away.

• Chapter 2 •

Cut of the Cards

HE TOOK HIS SOLITARY MEAL IN THE HOTEL DINING room. At this late hour there was little trade, and he was glad to be apart from others. He was a man whose thoughts always turned inward, for his profession kept him on a lonely path. There was that star upon which his eye was fixed, and he had learned one truism and kept carefully to it: the man traveled the fastest who traveled alone. Yet tonight he was acutely conscious when gay laughter lifted from a far table where a family took its meal; and he marked the comings and goings of pairs of people, wondering about them, wondering about their camaraderie.

Once he'd known the feeling of belonging, in the bunkhouses of far Texas, when he had been a working cowhand who had come to resent his station. That was when he had examined his skills and found only one that set him a notch above other men. His first gun job had been a little brawl along the Brazos, but there'd been a hefty bonus when the smoke cleared away, and he'd salted it down, every cent of it. Then those men from the big cattle interests in Wyoming had come recruiting for that Johnson County trouble, and he'd been aboard that special train that left Denver over the Union Pacific for northern Wyoming. He'd really made a name for himself at the siege on Crazy Woman Creek, even though the Wyoming invasion had turned into a debacle, with the United States Cavalry having to rescue the invaders.

Then he'd got a letter from Gault Telford and come farther north to sell his skill once again. But there was a perverseness in him that had made him hate his employers in Wyoming and take a sudden dislike to Telford. Some part of his convictions had been shaken tonight; and so he ate alone now, wondering about people from whom he had set himself apart, ordinary, unimportant people who laughed at their suppers.

When he had eaten, he came again to the lobby and found Rita there. She sat in one of the chairs, alongside her father, whose right hand was now wrapped in a bandage. Randall nudged the brim of his Stetson and gave Rita a smile. Rita's glance was straight, but she didn't smile back. Dan Saxon nodded, showing no malice; and Randall wondered how much of what had transpired upstairs Rita had told her father.

Randall said, "How's the hand?"

"A bad scratch," Saxon said.

"And when it's healed enough so you can handle a gun again?"

Saxon smiled. "I know an ace when I see one face up. I haven't got the card to buck it."

Randall smiled again at Rita. "Are you as wise as your father?"

The heat of anger showed in Rita's eyes. "Someday, somewhere, you'll meet a man who'll bring you to your knees. I hope I'm there when that day comes!"

Randall said gravely, "Perhaps."

He touched his hat brim again and went out into the

street. Around him, Sleeping Cat's night life swirled; he could hear the music of the saloons and the constant rumble of men's voices; and as he moved along the street, he had to elbow his way.

He wanted the feel of this town. He saw the horses at the hitch racks and memorized their brands without conscious intention; he saw the number of bearded, booted railroad workers and studied them as one breed of man studies another. A week's pay in their pants, and the lid lifted! They were like the cowhands and the trail drifters and the frock-coated gamblers, living one day at a time. Considering this, some of his surety returned, for he was a man with an eye on tomorrow.

He passed the mercantile and the blacksmith shop and a millinery, all dark at this hour. A single lantern glowed deep within the recesses of a livery stable; beyond this was Sleeping Cat's only brick building—the bank. He looked at the gold lettering on the bank's window, but Gault Telford's name wasn't there. Randall hadn't expected it would be. The Telfords always held to the center of the web, dark and quiet as spiders. He remembered what Telford had said about this being his town.

When he'd got as far as Doc Farrell's cottage, he crossed over and walked along the far side of the street. He walked slowly, wary always of the shadowy slots between buildings, wary of any man who looked at him twice. This was instinctive, this being constantly ready. Sometimes he grew weary of it.

Suddenly he thought of the bed in the hotel and wanted nothing so much as to be in that bed. He crossed over to the hotel and came into the lobby and found Rita still here. Now she was in a far corner, curled up in a chair and reading a Miles City newspaper. She looked like a half-dozing kitten, not conscious of his quiet appraisal. He at once looked about for Dan Saxon and found him at a table with two other men, poker chips before them and the cards spread out.

Saxon raised his bandaged hand in salute and called, "Want to sit in for some poker?"

Randall shook his head. "Not tonight."

"A friendly game for small stakes," Saxon said, an edge of insistence to his voice.

"I'm no hand at cards."

"Well," Saxon said, his smile a challenge, "I tried my luck at *your* game."

Randall came over and kicked out a chair and straddled it. "Deal me in," he said.

Saxon inclined his head toward the other two men. "This is Barney Shay, who runs the mercantile here, and George, his clerk. Gentlemen, I give you Long Tom Randall."

Shay was silver-haired and bloodless and looked like a New England tradesman; George was young and sallow and probably dying of consumption. Randall gave them a nod, and Saxon collected the loose cards and shuffled them. Saxon's hands fascinated Randall, for those hands were doing that for which they were best fitted. The bandage seemed to bother Saxon not at all; his hands were like sunlight flashing on the leaves of cottonwoods. He dealt, gave Randall his smile again, and said, "The chips cash in at two bits each."

Randall picked up his cards, thinking, What the hell! You shoot at the man in the afternoon and play penny-ante with him in the evening!

He won the first hand; the next two went to Barney Shay. George had a turn then, and Saxon raked in a pot or two. It was that kind of game, seesawing across the table with no man having any high moment and the whole thing dull and listless. Shay spoke no more than was necessary for the game; George was as taciturn. Only those flashing hands of Dan Saxon kept Randall interested. His eyes got heavy, and he wished again that he were in bed, but the game dragged on to the soft sound of chips clinking and the cards being slapped against the tabletop.

After a while Rita came from her far corner and stood at her father's shoulder, watching the play. She soon tired of standing and took a chair nearby, waiting out the game. Randall watched her from a corner of his eye, wondering how many evenings she had spent this way. His own father's weakness had been the jug, and he, too, remembered nights of waiting.

At eleven o'clock, Shay said, "That's enough for me."

Saxon said, his face bland, "You owe me two dollars and six bits, Barney. I'll take it out in trade."

Shay frowned. "Sorry about what I had to tell you today, Dan. Business is business."

George stood up, and the payoff was made, and when the two had gone, Shay giving Randall a cold hand and George a colder one, Saxon picked up the cards and began idly shuffling them. He looked like a man more asleep than awake; his eyelids were heavy and his actions slow. Randall pushed back his chair, making this first move of departure, and Saxon said casually, "Rita tells me you'd like a ranch of your own."

Randall said, "Who wouldn't?"

"Circle-S crowds up against the western hills," Saxon said. "We've got water and timber and good graze, and the stock is blooded. None of your longhorn strain. There's an indebtedness against the place, but this season could pay that off, with luck. Would such a ranch interest you, Randall? The thing's a good buy."

"At what price?"

"At the cut of the cards."

"I heard what that storekeeper said to you. Is your back that tight against the wall?"

Saxon was no longer sleepy or pretending to be. His actor's face was tight with strain. "I'm a gambling man, mister. I've let you in for a dull evening, but I can put an exciting finish to it. We cut the deck. High card and you own Circle-S."

"And if it's low card?"

"Then you go to work for me at forty a month. You'll be my man, not Gault Telford's."

Rita came out of her chair and to the table. "No, Dad!" she cried.

Dan Saxon looked up at her. "I tried my way; you tried yours. What else is left? Think, girl! What can we lose, really?"

Rita said, "I don't like it!"

Saxon looked at Long Tom Randall. "Will you try such a gamble?"

Randall said, "I was told tonight that the Saxons never cheat." His lips quirked. "I've watched your hands. You could make that deck do anything you wanted."

"Perhaps," Saxon said and his smile again held a challenge.

In Randall then was no thought of his own; he was a wary man suddenly shed of wariness; he was a practical man gone crazy. He'd known this Dan Saxon a very few hours, and he'd bested the man at their first meeting, but now he was possessed of the strange feeling that there could be no besting Saxon, not really. There was something in the man that could be budged no more than a mountain could be budged, a kind of strength that was greater than gun or fist or the moneyed strength of a Gault Telford. And so Randall said, "Shuffle those cards."

Saxon obeyed, his hands flashing again in the lamplight. Randall looked up at Rita then and said, "You cut the deck."

She was a ghost of a girl, the color gone from her face, the hope gone from her eyes. Then she steeled herself and reached out and cut the deck and let it lie.

Saxon said in an even voice, "You first, Mr. Randall."

Randall reached and cut quickly, exposing the five of spades.

"A low one," Saxon said in that same even voice. "I think I can beat it, friend."

He reached out and made his cut, and Randall thought then, Everything he's ever worked for! All he owns—all his years! Dan exposed the three of diamonds. He looked at the card and tossed it down; and in that breathless moment, Rita sobbed. Saxon looked across the table at Randall and said, "It seems that you own a ranch."

"Yes," Randall said. "I own a ranch. I've beat you and you've beat Gault Telford. That's what you meant when you told your girl there was nothing to lose, eh?"

"Exactly," Saxon said.

Randall stood up. "Just one question: high card would have given you the ranch—and me. I still think you could have made that deck dance to your tune. Why didn't you do it?"

Saxon smiled his smile and held up his right hand so that the bandage showed. "You shot me, remember? I'm a clumsy man tonight."

In the morning Randall rented a horse from the livery stable he had marked the night before and rose westward over a fair, bright land that was dew-drenched and undulating and reached to the far hills. The grass was lush here, lusher range than he had known in Texas or Wyoming, good range with good cattle feeding upon it and only a few fences to mar its expanse. He rode easily and unhurried, liking being back in a saddle again. He rode alone in the great bowl of Sleeping Cat Basin, with the sky arching above him and only a few fleecy clouds showing and the pine-strippled hills drawing ever nearer. Meadow larks made their morning music, and he was glad to be rid of the ugliness of the town.

Such cattle as he saw interested him. He'd been told that a few years ago you could find every kind of cattle in Montana—lean longhorns that poured up from Texas, a strain sometimes mixed with shorthorn blood from Missouri herds; pilgrim or barnyard cattle from the farms of Michigan, Minnesota, Wisconsin; cattle driven eastward out of Oregon and Washington and Idaho to overstock the ranges. But since that disastrous hard winter of five years before, the wiser operators had gone in for limited range and supplemental feeding, smaller herds and better ones. Now you found a native stock that was gold on the hoof. Randall liked the looks of the cattle.

He was on his way to Circle-S, and he had his directions from the livery stable man. He might have ridden out with the Saxons, for he supposed they'd be heading for the ranch this morning, but he liked being alone. Moreover, there was still a slight resentment in him toward Dan Saxon, the resentment of being born too late to be a cattle king, born to a rigged world where the masters of many acres stayed masters and the lesser men rode for them. A cut of the cards had changed all that, yet the feeling was strong in him that somehow the victory had gone to Dan Saxon, who had moulded him, Long Tom Randall, to his own needs.

Once Randall had seen a Texas cowhand fashion the clay of a creek bank into a horse. It had been no such horse as mortal man had ever ridden, but it was a horse to its creator's fancy.

Considering this, he came across the miles with the sun mounting higher until summer's full fury was on the basin and the livery stable horse was patched with sweat and Randall's shirt stuck to his shoulders. But presently he began to laugh. You met a man and swapped shots with him. You met his daughter and had her throw herself at you. Then you were cutting a deck of cards and tipping your Stetson and saying good night to the two of them, and now you were riding across your own acreage with the sweat running down your back. For now he had passed through Circle-S's gate.

Within the hour he came upon the ranch buildings, a log and frame scatteration of structures shoved up against the base of the western hills.

He looked at these buildings, thinking, They're mine! but he couldn't yet grasp the reality of it. He looked at the great, gaunt ranchhouse and the low, sod-roofed bunkhouse and the barn and corrals and blacksmith shop and other buildings. Smoke lifted from the cook shack, but otherwise the place had a deserted look. A few saddlers stomped in the corrals, switching idly at flies; no man showed himself in the yard.

Randall stepped down from the rented horse and led it to the watering trough, letting it drink a little at a time. He stripped the gear from the mount and turned the horse into one of the corrals and hung the saddle over a corral pole. Then he came toward the ranchhouse and climbed to the shade of the long gallery fronting the place. He saw that the ranchhouse windows had heavy shutters, scarred and pitted. Looking closer, he found a flint arrowhead imbedded in one. He had come from Texas where the Comanches had raided when the moon was full and the desert waterholes brimmed, but Indian wars were to him part of the tales of useless old men. He realized now how old this Circle-S ranchhouse must be.

Then the door opened, and Rita stood there. She surveyed him in a cool, detached way and said, "Don't you want to come in?" Her voice was cool, soft.

He'd got such an early start that he'd supposed he must be ahead of the Saxons. Yet Rita was here; and when he came into the ranchhouse, he found Dan Saxon awaiting him, a day's stubble of beard on his aristocratic face. Never had Saxon looked more like a cattle king—yet he was now a cattle king who no longer owned a single cow. It was the room, the setting, that gave Saxon his air of whang-leather grandeur; it was a big room with handhewn, smoke-blackened rafters and a huge stone fireplace at the far end. The scattered furniture had been built to last; the room looked serviceable rather than comfortable.

Randall said with faint irony, "I saw the arrowhead outside. You forgot to mention Indians when you were bragging last night about all that went with this ranch."

Saxon said, "It's been a long time since there was any real trouble. But the first few years we slept with loaded rifles by our bunks. We were burnt out twice. I left that arrowhead in the shutter to remind me that I must always stand guard. First it was Indians; then it was rustlers."

Randall's face puckered, and he thought, He's trying to tell me something. But he wasn't sure what Saxon meant. Still, he knew the thrust of compassion, thinking that here was a man who had fought to hold his own and that now it was lost to him. He didn't want that compassion to show, but it must have, for Saxon shrugged slightly and spread his hands in the way of a gambler whose luck has run against him.

"We came out here to get our personal belongings," he said. "We'll be off the place before sundown."

"No," Randall said. "You're not going."

"It's your home now. The county seat is fifty miles beyond Sleeping Cat, but I'll pass through there on my way out of the country. The matter of the deed can be taken care of then. I'll see to it."

Randall shook his head. "You're staying here to work for me."

Saxon's lips quirked. "That wasn't in the bargain, my friend."

Rita said in a sarcastic voice, "Don't you see, Dad? He wants the tables turned. He wants the rancher working for forty a month for a change."

Randall flashed her a smile. "That's the pay. You named it yourself, girl. Last night, Remember?"

Saxon said, "We're heading for St. Louis."

"Not yet," Randall said. "There's those cows to be

got to the railroad camp. That's the way this place gets back on its feet and Telford gets trounced. You mentioned the indebtedness last night; Telford told me about your way out. You know your stock; you know the country. I don't. So I need your kind of savvy to make the delivery. That's why you're staying."

Saxon seated himself in a rawhide-bottomed chair. "A crew goes with the place. And a foreman. His name is Curly Mather. I think you saw him in Sleeping Cat."

"The man who came running up after I shot you? Riders come a dime a dozen, and he didn't look too bright to me. We'll need him and the others, but we'll need you more. You're going to stay, mister."

Saxon's face stiffened. "What makes you think so?"

"Because you want Gault Telford beat. Because that was all that was left you when you talked about cutting the cards. You were seeing this place slip through your fingers anyway, so it pleased you to have it go to a man who would buck Telford—the very man Telford had brought in to beat you. *Me*. But the game isn't won, not if Telford shows up here to claim a busted ranch. You wouldn't want that. So that's why you'll stay, mister, at forty a month and chuck. You'll stay because, as much as you likely hate me, you hate Telford more."

He looked straight at Saxon, trying to read the man, but Saxon's face was schooled. Then Saxon grinned and shrugged, and that was his surrender. "You've seen through me," he said. "Yes, I'll stay."

"Then move your stuff out to the bunkhouse," Randall said. "You're one of the hands now."

Saxon inclined his head toward Rita, who'd stood listening. "And her?"

"She'll have to be part of the bargain I've driven with you. I know that. So she can go on being queen of the castle. Just see that she keeps out of the way of working men."

Rita said in a low, even voice, "You're absolutely insufferable!"

Randall turned to her. "I spoke my piece to you last night. That was only half of it. You folks handed me a ranch on a platter, but it happens to be a mighty hot platter. Nobody's going to make me let loose of it before it cools off—not you or Gault Telford or your father or the crew that rides for this spread. Nobody! I've got me a ranch, but it won't really be mine till it's in the clear. I'll wring the last ounce of sweat out of every man, dog and horse on this spread to make that possible. You're staying here because I need your father. And for no other reason. No man, no woman, nothing will stop me from breaking any hold Telford has on this place. Do you savvy?"

Rita looked at him, and the anger left her eyes and was replaced by a remote sadness. "I told you once I should be sorry for you," she said. "Now I'm wondering if I shouldn't be sorry for Sleeping Cat. I think we've traded one Gault Telford for another."

The sternness left Randall and he grinned. "Maybe you have," he said.

He faced Dan Saxon again. "Tell me how the work's coming?"

"We've been making an off-season gather," Saxon said. "It amounts to a fall roundup held early. It will be finished in another week; the crew's out working at it now. From that gather we'll cut prime beef, because the grading crew contractor demands it. Then we'll trail it to the camp."

"How far to where the crew is working? I want to talk to them."

"You won't have to ride out. They're bedding the gather close to the ranch, and they'll be coming in for their noon meal any time now."

"I'll be waiting for them," Randall said.

It was cool here in the semidarkness of this big room, and it was a pleasant place when a man got used to the size of it. But he strode out to the gallery again and stood there, putting his shoulder to a porch support and fashioning up a cigarette. He looked beyond the yard, watching for a dust cloud to show itself, watching for the first sign of approaching riders. But his thoughts were elsewhere. Something nagged at his consciousness, something having to do with that Indian arrowhead and what Saxon had tried to tell him without putting it into words.

He finished his quirly and got out his jackknife and went to the shutter and dug out the arrowhead. It lay in his palm, an ugly reminder of savagery. He turned it over in his palm and rubbed a thumb across the rough flint surface. Then he frowned and flung the arrowhead far out into the yard.

Just then the crew came riding up.

There were six of them, and he supposed that a couple more had been left with the gathered beef, making at least eight in all. The old ones, the grizzled ones, were Texans, men who'd come up the trail with Saxon, he supposed. The younger ones had a salty look to them, too. He weighed them and measured them with his glance, wanting to know how much leather was in them, wanting to know how they'd stand when Telford made a play. Then they were into the yard, stirring up a maelstrom of dust as they came to a stop and some stepped down from their saddles. He at once recognized Mather, remembering him from Sleeping Cat. He saw that Mather recognized him, too, for Mather tossed his reins to one of the younger men and came toward the gallery, frowning.

Randall was at once wary and at once ready, knowing instantly that here was the one who would give him trouble.

Dan Saxon came out of the house and stood behind Randall's right shoulder; Randall was conscious of his being there and knew an old squeamishness at having a man behind his back. He was thinking that Saxon might have come to regret the bargain of the cards, and thus he was acutely aware that he was now whipsawed between Saxon and Saxon's crew. But Saxon, scarcely raising his voice, said, "Boys, this is Long Tom Randall, the new owner. You'll be taking your orders from him." He threw the words out to the crew and let them lie.

Curly Mather stopped in midstride. He stood peering from under his hatbrim, a tall man, tall almost as Randall, a slab-muscled man, a weather-burned man, the product of a hard era, a hard way of life. His solid features showed his astonishment; he had the look of not believing what his ears had told them. He said then, quickly, "The hell you say!"

Edgy, Randall thought. Talks first and thinks afterwards, and he knew then how Mather must be handled.

Saxon said, "Sorry, Curly, but it's so."

The rest of the crew waited, coming down from saddles and forming a solid body behind Mather to make restless movements of hands and feet. From Mather they took their day's orders; to Mather they gave loyalty and obedience, and these things were ingrained and had become tradition, a part of cattledom. To them Curly Mather was now a weather vane, and they would turn whichever way the wind blew him. This, too, Randall recognized; and he looked at the old, guarded faces and the young, taut faces and knew that the things they understood were the hard hand and the quick quirt. They were a breed that prized its independence and recognized only the rawest strength; he knew them full well, for he had been born to their breed.

That was why he said, "Nothing's changed, boys. You've got the same job with the same brand at the same pay. Now get your grub and get back to work."

Mather's face stayed unyielding. "I'm not working for any damn' gun-slick!"

Randall cleared the gallery steps without touching them. He made the jump and lunged across the open to

Mather so suddenly as to give the foreman no warning. He came at Mather with his right fist looping up; his knuckles struck hard at Mather's jaw. Too late, Mather saw the blow coming and frantically pulled his head aside. Randall's fist glánced, but Mather's wild defensive move threw the foreman off balance, and he went down. Randall towered over him, putting his boot against Mather's chest and putting the weight of his body upon his right leg, pinning Mather down.

Randall said through his teeth, "You're a hired man. You'll never be anything but somebody's hired man. You can be mine, or you can ride out. Now get to your feet and make up your mind!"

He stepped back from Mather, and the man put the heel of his hand to the ground and levered himself upward to an awkward stand. Death was in his eyes; they held Randall and tore Randall to pieces, and then Mather's stare shifted beyond Randall to the gallery.

Randall said, "Well, are you staying?"

Mather was still looking beyond Randall, looking, Randall supposed, at Dan Saxon. Randall wanted mightily to turn his head, but he knew better. Only so long as he faced Mather could he hope to dominate Mather, and Mather was now making his fight with himself; it showed in his face.

Mather said then, "I'll stay."

Randall said, "If there's anything still stuck in your craw, get it out!"

Mather's face worked, the hate alive in his eyes. "Just don't ever lay a hand on me again!"

"That will be up to you," Randall said. His glance moved from Mather to the men behind the foreman. "Anybody else got anything to say?"

Again there was that restless movement of hands and feet, and the animosity that rose from the bunch was almost tangible; Randall felt its weight. When he had humbled Mather, he had humbled all of them and earned their hatred, yet by this same token Mather had answered for all of them. Someone made a move to lead a horse toward the corral. Another followed him, and another, and thus they signified their intent; they would stick. Mather was the last to move away. He gave Randall the fullness of his malevolence in a final glance and headed across the yard. Only then did Randall look toward the gallery. Dan Saxon stood there, a silent spectator to all that had happened, his face showing nothing. Beside him stood Rita.

Randall looked up at her. "So it was you told Mather to stay."

Rita said, "I told him nothing. But if I'd nodded my head, he'd have ridden out. I like it better that he is staying. If there's one man here who may cut you down to size, it's Curly. Sooner or later you'll push him too far."

"Maybe," Randall said.

He took a hipshot stand and watched the crew drift from the corrals to the cook shack. He remembered that he was very hungry, and he walked to the cook shack, waited his turn and gave his face a *whoosh* from the wash basin on the bench outside the door. He entered the shack to find most of the crew already seated around a long table, Mather among them. The cook was filling plates, and Randall sized him up and judged that he would be an additional fighting man in a pinch. Telford, who'd tried to hire a Long Tom Randall, would hire others; and some dark night Telford would strike at Circle-S.

An empty chair stood at the head of the table, and Randall knew this must be Dan Saxon's. Dan and Rita entered, and Randall became conscious that every eye was on him. He walked to the head of the table, got behind the chair and hauled it out. He looked at Rita. "Here," he invited.

For a moment she hesitated, not knowing how to interpret his act, and Randall kept his face bland. She smiled and came to the chair and let him seat her, and she whispered, "Thanks."

He bent to her ear. "Why not?" he asked, low-voiced. "You kept the crew here for me."

Anger colored her cheeks. "I did nothing for *you*! Please understand that!"

He said, keeping a straight face, "If you want to shoot me, I'll loan you my gun."

Then he found an empty chair for himself and fell to eating. Outwardly he paid no heed to the crew, yet he was keenly alert; and he noticed that the talk was stiff and desultory, having none of the usual camaraderie of a ranch meal. Once he looked across at Dan Saxon, who was poker-stiff, but the glint of laughter was in his eyes.

After the meal, Randall drifted out into the yard with the crew, cut out a Circle-S horse from the corral, put a saddle on it and rode with Mather and the others. They paralleled the hills, moving southward for a mile and more, and shortly they came upon the beef gather, a great brown blotch upon the grass. A couple of men squatted in the skimpy shade of their ground-anchored horses, watching. At a nod from Mather, these two rose to leather and headed toward the ranch for their noon meal.

Randall rode close to Mather. "How's it coming?"

Mather's lips thinned down, but he spoke in a civil voice. "We've combed most of the draws. Another week and we'll start cutting out what we're trailing to the railroad. The boys know their job and they know the country. If you want to see how we operate, trail along with anyone you choose."

He rode away from Randall and began giving orders to the men; at once there was a great show of confusion, but out of the seeming chaos came orderly activity. Two men were delegated to stay with the herd, spelling the two who'd headed to the ranch. The new pair went to a wagon and got firewood from it and started building a branding fire. Their job would be to brand and earmark the summer calves that had come since the spring round-up. The others got fresh horses from the small, rope-corralled remuda and began to diverge, the riders spreading fanwise.

Randall nudged his horse and attached himself to an oldtimer, a grizzled one who rode southward until the herd was lost from sight. The oldster headed into a draw. Randall trailed silently behind him. When the draw split, two wooded thumbs digging at angles into the hills, the old fellow cocked an eye at Randall.

"Be you a cowboy?"

Randall nodded. "Starting today."

"I'm Pecos," said the old-timer.

"It's a good name."

"I'll take this here right hand draw. You want to help, you find yourself any cows that's up the other draw, then chouse 'em toward the bedding ground."

"At a walk? Or shall I run hell out of 'em?" His eyes bored the mossyhorn.

Pecos squinted hard, but Randall kept his face innocent. Pecos grinned, and with that grin a friendship was forged. "You go to hell," Pecos said affably and headed up the right hand draw.

Whereupon Randall rode alone, following the draw in its gentle climb upward. Another mile into the hills, he came upon three steers bearing the Circle-S brand. He got these to drifting down the draw and rode on. He found himself liking this work; it was like going back to a remembered place and thereby dissolving all the years since he'd last looked upon it. He liked the sky over him and the saddle leather under him; he liked the demand upon a skill he had long forsaken. He grew prideful of the task.

When the draw sprouted fingers, he explored each one meticulously and found a couple more steers which he started downhill, being careful not to run the tallow off them. Then, in the far reaches, he found a mossyhorn, an ancient bunch-quitter that had eluded many roundups and grown wild as any wolf. Randall was glad he was aboard a Circle-S horse rather than the livery stable mount. The horse had savvy, but the mossyhorn was elusive, and the chase led through pine thickets and deep brush and called for all of Randall's riding skill. Presently he found himself cussing that perverse steer with considerable heat. At last he got the mossyhorn headed downhill; but here was a born bunch-quitter, quick to turn at any time, and he herded it out of many corners before he descended to the place where he had left Pecos.

It was then the accident happened.

The scrap of paper might have come from a letter some cowhand had dropped, or it might have been the label from a can. It had caught on a bush, and Randall hadn't noticed it on the ride up, but now it fluttered in the breeze. Randall's horse laid back its ears, shied and caught him napping. He tried frantically to clamp leather with his knees and turn his toes inward to lock himself in the saddle; and then in a wild moment of realization that he was off balance, he kicked free of the stirrups. He contrived to land on his shoulder and at once rolled away from the rearing horse, but the steer turned and came at him. He wasn't prepared for that. A longhorn would inevitably charge an unhorsed rider, but this was native stock, a gentler breed. But this steer was coming on with lowered head. Randall tried to get at his gun, but his holster had been twisted awry by the fall.

He was on one knee when a rider cut between him and the steer, snapping at the mossyhorn with a rope end, turning the brute.

Pecos! he thought and was weak with relief.

He got up, caught at the reins of his horse and was at once into the saddle, and safe. He saw then that the rider was Rita—Rita in jeans and sombrero and denim shirt.

He said, "What the hell are you doing out here?"

She had got the steer loping on down the trail. She drew up beside Randall and said, "Earning my keep. I've choused out seven cows this afternoon. How well have you done?" She was breathing hard; her face, flushed by exertion and excitement, was startlingly alive, startlingly pretty.

He shook his head. "It's no game for a girl."

"I've ridden in roundups before! Whenever I chose to. You told dad this morning why you were keeping him. I was supposed to be a free boarder who went along with the bargain. You have your kind of pride, friend, but you never stop to think whether anyone else has theirs. If I eat Circle-S grub, I do Circle-S work!"

He plucked that fluttering bit of paper from the bush and balled it tightly in his fist. "You saved my life," he said.

"Anybody—Curly, even—would have done the same under the circumstances."

"I wonder," he said.

She spun her horse about. "We're wasting time. There are cows to be gathered."

Then she was spurring down the trail, gone about her work. He watched her ride away, and he said softly, aloud, "Well I'll be damned!" Then he threw back his head and his laughter came and was caught by the hills and sent echoing.

• Chapter 3 •

Dark Shadow

There were to be many more days to the round-up—days of awakening to the cook's alarm clock set on an overturned dishpan to make a greater racket, days of taking the early morning kinks out of saddlers and combing the far draws to build the beef gather. Rita rode with the crew through those days, as did Saxon, both of them turning in full measures of work. Dust rose and the acrid odor of singed hair and flesh was in the air, and the mingled blatting of branded calves and concerned mother cows made a constant cacaphony. Men grew gaunt from toil and short of temper, but still the work went on. At night while the stars stood out and the coyotes mourned in the high hills, the bedded herd lay lulled by the old Texas songs as the night-hawks rode their endless circles.

"Forty a month an' chuck-wagon grub,
Forty a month and found.

Oh, think of the joys of a cowboy's life
While you're ridin' the old bed-ground. . . .''

Randall took his turn at the nighthawking, and on his off-nights slept at the ranchhouse, usurping Dan Saxon's bedroom while Rita slept across the hall from him, and her father retired to the bunkhouse. Curly Mather raised an objection to this arrangement the first night.

''You mean you're staying alone in the house with Rita?'' he demanded of Randall.

They were on the gallery, Rita and Randall and Saxon, the men having an after-supper smoke; and Mather had joined them here, come to talk over tomorrow's work. Through the day he had been a tractable man, who had gone about his work with efficiency, proving himself a good hand with cattle. There had been a stiff restraint in his few contacts with Randall, but not till now had he raised a personal issue. Mather was a good foreman, Randall had decided.

Now Randall looked at him and smiled a slow smile. ''Rita won't do me no harm.''

Mather made a big, solid shape in the darkness of the gallery. ''Damn it!'' he snapped. ''That isn't what I meant.''

Randall said with no rancor, ''The ranchhouse is mine. She can sleep here if she chooses. Or she can go to the bunkhouse or the barn.''

''Look,'' Mather argued, ''in the name of common decency, it shouldn't be her that moves out of the house.''

''Never mind, Curly,'' Rita interjected wearily. ''I'll lock my door.''

''Just the same,'' Mather said hotly, ''I'm unrolling my soogans right here on the gallery. I'll be within shouting distance if you need me, Rita.''

''What happens if it's *me* that starts bellowing for help?'' Randall asked placidly.

He'd been watching Mather closely, and he saw the man take a step forward with his fist cocked; but Rita said sharply, ''Forget it, Curly!''

"I've spoke my piece," Mather said stubbornly.

Thus it came about that Mather spread his blankets on the gallery each evening, while Randall and Rita retired to the house. The crew made a great pretense of ignoring this nightly ritual of Mather's; but Dan Saxon sometimes smiled when, leaving the house at an evening's end, he had to step over the foreman to get from the gallery.

No more was said about the subject, but Mather was still in charge of the roundup; and whenever it was his own turn to do the nighthawk's trick, he named Randall as his partner, keeping the two of them away from the ranchhouse at the same time. They rode the long circles, passing each other in sullen silence till the watch was done. On the other nights, Randall lay in the dark house, strongly conscious of Rita's nearness. He had thought her to be a cattle king's spoiled darling and he had resented her with the resentment he gave to all those in the high places. Now he knew that she could turn in a day's work. She was a paradox to him; but she was also a woman, dark and smiling and making a strong call to an unnamed hunger in the stillness of the nights. . . .

By the week's end the gather was finished, and Randall asked Dan Saxon to direct the cutting. Through the herd Saxon rode, pointing out the prime beef, while men on cutting horses crisscrossed the gather, chousing out the cows Saxon had indicated. He chose the very best beef for this first delivery; a good showing would net Circle-S the contract to supply beef as long as the construction crews were in the hills. A couple of the men would stay behind when the trail drive started, their job being to let the rest of the herd graze over a wide area yet keep them out of the hills so the whole round-up would not have to be repeated if the drovers came back from the railroad spur with an immediate order for more beef.

They got the trail herd selected by the end of that

day, a few hundred prime head. They decided to make the start the next morning, but when the time came they learned of a difficulty none had anticipated. The coosie, a sour and forthright man, told them. "There ain't enough grub," he said.

"But I got a wagonload from Barney Shay," Dan Saxon pointed out.

"We've been eating off that for a week," the cook reminded him. "By my calculations, it will take another week to get those cows to the railroad. We can't go that far on what's left. You want a chuck wagon on this drive, you better get something to put inside it."

Saxon frowned. "Shay closed down the lid after that last load."

Randall, who'd heard all this, said, "That's my problem now." He turned to the coosie. "Make out a list of what you'll need—everything from Arbuckle's coffee on through the alphabet. The others can start pushing the herd along. Where's Pecos? He can start to town right now with a wagon. I'll follow him with the coosie's list and arrange for the grub. We can catch up with you."

And so it was that when the herd, fashioned into the shape of a blunt arrowhead, was pointed toward the higher hills, men at point and swing and eating the dust of the drag, Long Tom Randall rode in the opposite direction, rode toward Sleeping Cat, leading the horse he'd rented from the livery stable. Pecos, with the wagon, had an hour's start, and Randall was almost to town before he overtook the man. He paced the wagon then, and rider and rig came into Sleeping Cat together, Pecos pulling the wagon up before the mercantile store.

"Wait here," Randall said and jangled his spurs inside. The store was empty of customers, but Randall found George here and behind the counter, his other erstwhile companion of the poker table, Barney Shay. This bloodless man greeted him with a careful howdy. Randall laid the cook's list before him and said, "You can put this stuff in the wagon outside."

Shay pushed his steel-rimmed spectacles down on his nose, cleared his throat twice, then said, "We run a strictly cash business."

"In a cowtown?" Randall asked wryly. "Do the ranchers hereabouts drive one cow to market everytime they want to trade with you?"

"Cash is our rule."

"Okay," said Randall, "I've got the cash. It's in a Denver bank. Will you take an order on that bank?"

"The rule is cash on the counter."

Randall stared at this man and understood then, for it was as though the dark shadow of Gault Telford lay across the pinched features of Barney Shay. Randall had expected an attack on Circle-S, and in the long night watches he had quickened to all alien sounds in the darkness, anticipating a raid. But this was Telford's way of closing out Circle-S, this shadowy way. He, Randall, had thought that Telford would strike with guns, but the Telfords shied from violence until no other way was left but violence. Telford had merely passed the word to Shay, and Shay was adamant. It was as simple as that.

Something stirred in Randall then that edged his voice. "My men aren't going hungry because of your damn' rule!" His own words sounded queer to him until he thought about them. *My men,* he'd said. That was the Circle-S bunch he'd bullied into submission by bullying Curly Mather, that bunch with whom he'd ridden and worked for only one short week. But the responsibility of feeding them had come also with the cut of the cards, and now he reached and got a grip on Barney Shay's shirt and drew the man halfway across his own counter. "Now get at that loading!" he insisted.

"George!" Shay squawked.

The consumptive George had been making a great business of plying a broom in a far corner. He looked toward his employer; he looked as though he were about to burst into tears. Then he said, "I'm not bucking *him.*"

Shay's hands flailed at Randall. "Let me go! You can have the grub!"

"Get to loading it then!" He released Shay.

Shay took the list and turned to the shelves and began piling canned goods upon the counter. George carried load after load of merchandise out to the wagon. Randall leaned against a crackerbarrel, his arms folded, and merely watched, shaking his head when Pecos came in and made a move to help with the loading. Between them, Shay and George got the last item into the wagon, and when this was done Randall waved a hand at Pecos. "Get started," he said.

Pecos gone, Randall said, "Fetch me pen and ink. I'll draw up an order on that Denver bank."

He did this, then walked from the mercantile, leaving a heavy silence behind him. He took the spare horse back to the livery stable and paid for its use. He came again to the street and stood on the edge of the boardwalk and rolled up a cigarette. Presently he began to laugh. He was thinking: I never even lifted my gun from leather; and he was remembering George's frantic, "I'm not bucking *him*." Sometimes he'd hated being a legend, but today he'd laid his own dark shadow, and it had been greater than Telford's. He thought about that and knew why Curly Mather hadn't come to his feet fighting that day they'd tangled at Circle-S.

He finished his quirly and was putting his boot heel to it when a boy came along the street and said, "Mr. Telford wants to see you."

Randall looked solemnly at the urchin. "Mr. Telford break a leg?"

"He's waiting in his office. He said he'd be pleased if you'd drop in."

Shay had likely run blubbering to his master, Randall reflected. But he crossed over in the direction the boy indicated and came to a small frame building set down upon the main street, a building so unpretentious that he had paid it no heed that night he'd walked this street. He came through an open doorway into a dimly-lighted office, its air heavy with the piled-up heat of the day. In the semigloom he made out a squat iron safe, a few chairs, and a rolltop desk. In a creaking swivel chair before the desk sat Gault Telford, smiling benignly.

There were three other men in the room, silent men, truculent men, one standing against each wall, with folded arms. Randall gave them his quick appraisal and his contempt; they were of the tumbleweed breed, hard-fisted and slow-thinking and for sale always at bargain prices.

"Who are the boys?" he asked.

"Friends," Telford said. "Sit down, Tom. All I want is five minutes of your time."

"I can manage to stand that long."

Telford's smile spread and seemed to encompass the room. "I've heard tell that you won Circle-S on the cut of a deck of cards. Is that true?"

"True."

"Have you got the papers? You know that a gambling debt isn't legal and can't be collected in a Montana court of law, don't you?"

Randall hadn't known this, but he said, "Isn't that my worry?"

"Yes, it is," Telford conceded. He made a spreading gesture with his hands. "Look, Tom, it is time this foolishness ended. I'll concede that you are at least the present owner of Circle-S. What is your price to sell to me and leave this part of the country?"

"I like ranching."

Telford's eyes hardened behind those thick glasses. "That's your answer? Your final answer?"

"That's right."

Telford sighed; he looked like a man distressed by contemplating what he must do. He lifted his hand high, and Randall recognized the gesture as a signal. Randall had been watching the silent three set like so many wooden cigar store Indians. Too late, he anticipated the fourth man, the one who must have been posted outside and who responded to Telford's signal by stepping in through the open doorway behind Randall and wrapping an arm around Randall's throat, closing the arm sharply, elbow out.

Telford cried shrilly, "Get his gun!"

Randall felt the gun plucked from his holster; he heard it clatter to the floor. He bent forward, trying to throw his assailant over his head. At once the other three were closing in; one slammed at Randall's jaw with a fist; another planted a kick in Randall's stomach. He went down then, writhing in pain, and all four were upon him, striking and kicking. He fought back at them, knowing the futility of fighting against such odds but wanting to get in a few licks. He struggled to his feet, only to be borne down by the sheer weight of the four. Flame exploded in his brain and blackness came after it, and his last consciousness was of Telford leaning forward in his chair watching all this, an intent look on his face, an eagerness in his eyes.

He came from the darkness of oblivion to find himself in the darkness of night, the hard ground under him and the stars wheeling high above. His first real awareness was of pain; pain was everywhere, running through all his muscles and clouding his thinking and making him wish for unconsciousness. Groaning, he closed his eyes again. Someone began tugging at his armpits, trying to get him to a stand. He fought feebly, not wanting to be moved, since it hurt to be moved. He cursed the man whose persistent hands kept at him; he wanted that man to go away.

Reality came back with a rush, and he remembered the beating he'd taken in Telford's office and knew then that he had been tossed into a back alley of Sleeping Cat like some common drunk. He recalled Telford's sadistic pleasure; and anger became a white flame, obliterating pain, but only for a moment. Pain was a giant holding him tightly and warding off all else. He ceased fighting the man who was tugging at him.

"You've got to get up on your laigs!" the man urged desperately; and Randall recognized the voice. It was Pecos.

Randall made the try, and with Pecos' help he got to a tottering stand. Yonder the sounds of Sleeping Cat rose to the sky—the beat of boots along the boardwalk, the wildness of a piano in some saloon, the lifted shout of a drunken cowpoke. Back here there was darkness and silence and pain. The flame of anger still flickered, and Randall said, "Give me your gun!"

Pecos was a murky silhouette. "Your own's in your holster."

Randall felt and found it so, but the movement hurt. He began exploring himself for broken bones and found none. Nausea moved through him in a compelling wave, and he tottered toward the rear of the nearest building, put his hand to its rough wall for support, and vomited. He stood for a moment, sick and weak, but his head was clearer. It struck him then that Pecos was supposed to be halfway across Sleeping Cat Basin with a load of grub. Damn it all, the crew needed that grub! He spoke of this to Pecos.

"I got worried when you didn't come loping along after me," Pecos explained. "The fu'ther I got, the more worried I got. Finally I turned back. Nobody seemed to have seen you; nobody knew nothin' about you. But I found your horse tied up, so I knew you was still here. I kept lookin'."

"Where's the wagon now?"

Pecos gestured. "Edge of town."

"Let's get into it."

He was thinking with sudden panic that it would be too bad if Telford's men found that wagon and removed the grub. He took a step and almost fell. Pecos was at once steadying him, and they moved along the alley with Randall lurching and staggering. At times his anger overrode his pain, and in such moments his thought was to go seeking Telford and his plug-uglies, yet common sense told him there had to be another day for that. They got to the outskirts of town, and there Randall perceived the outlines of the wagon and team. His own saddler had been hitched to the tailgate, but the horse looked twenty feet high.

"I'll ride in the wagon a piece," he said.

Pecos at once clambered into the wagon and began rearranging supplies. He worked at this for many minutes, while Randall leaned against a wagon wheel. "Only got one blanket here," Pecos announced. "I've made room for you and spread it out. Climb in."

Randall set his right boot to the wheel hub and reached with his right hand for a grip on the wagon box and started pulling himself upward. Pain lanced the length of his right arm and spread through his body, and for a moment he was sure he was going to faint. Pecos reached from the wagon and grasped at him, and Randall gritted his teeth and fought the pain, and in this manner he was tumbled into the wagon. He fell upon the blanket and rolled over and put his back to it.

Pecos looked at him in the starlight, the oldster's lined face showing concern. "There's a sawbones in town. Fellow named Farrell. I'd best git you to him."

"No!" Randall said. "Get this wagon moving!"

"You wait a minute," Pecos said.

He hopped out of the wagon and started off toward town, and Randall called after him, "I don't want a doctor!" He didn't know whether Pecos heard him or would heed him if he did, and he cursed Pecos for a blundering fool. If a doctor came, all the tale would be told in Sleeping Cat before another sunset. And that tale mustn't be told, not the whole of it anyway, not the fact that Long Tom Randall's gun arm had been beaten and stomped upon until it was nearly useless.

For that was the bitter truth he had to contemplate

now as he waited for Pecos. He had had one skill that set him above other men, one stock in trade; and it had made him a legend, the kind of legend that Curly Mather had been afraid to buck hard, the kind of legend that had scared Barney Shay and George into loading this wagon with grub. But those four plug-uglies of Telford's, with their angry fists and boots, had made him a shorn Samson, and the restoring of his gun to its holster had been the last ironic touch before they'd heaved him into an alley. And now he could only lie here and curse them till his breath was spent, curse them and hope that no doctor would come to gauge the real extent of the damages.

At least no bones had been broken. But his muscles had been pounded and stomped until the resiliency was gone from them. He supposed that time would heal him, but he wondered how long it would take. A week? Two weeks? He grew fretful and worried over what was keeping Pecos. And then he heard Pecos returning.

The old-timer had fetched a pint of whiskey, and this he handed silently to Randall. Randall got the bottle to his lips with an effort and put his teeth to the cork. He let the whiskey run freely; it warmed his stomach and numbed the pain, and the world was less dark than it had been.

Pecos peered at him in the starlight. "How many of 'em was there?"

"Four. Telford was there, too, damn him, but he only watched."

"They didn't mark your face much."

Randall managed a wry grin. "It wasn't my good looks they were trying to spoil."

Pecos shook his head. "No, I reckon it wouldn't be that."

Again the whole horrible realization of his impotency rose to smite Randall, and fear put an edge to anger. He tried to raise his right arm, but pain gave him a sharp reminder of its uselessness, so he raised his left instead. He got his hand on Pecos' shirtfront, and he said, "Circle-S isn't to know about this—not all of it, anyway! Do you understand? I got in a saloon fight and got roughed up a little. Something like that. But you're telling no one that I couldn't lift myself into this wagon! That clear, you damn' old fool?"

Pecos said, "Now who the hell would I be telling?"

Randall let go of the man. "I'm sorry. You'd better start this wagon moving."

"Sure," Pecos said. "Those boys may be a mite hungry by the time we catch up with 'em."

Randall said, "You're a mighty good man, Pecos."

Pecos grunted, clambered to the wagon seat and shook out the reins, and the wagon began moving westward. At once it was a jolting rock, making a bed of torture for Randall. He moved himself about, trying to find a position a little more comfortable; he closed his eyes and set his teeth against the pain.

He was to remember that ride always, himself flat on his back, with the stars blurring above him and the constant *clop-clop* of the horses' hoofs in his ears. At times he was certain he would find it less painful aboard the saddler, and he was of a mind to ask Pecos to stop the wagon and help him mount the trailing horse. At times he fainted, and these were the blessed moments, bringing him oblivion, bringing him surcease from pain. He nipped at the whiskey bottle sparingly, but he had drained it long before they reached Circle-S's acreage.

The hours were endless hours, the miles were endless miles. By tipping his head far back, Randall could see Pecos upon the seat; but even such effort cost him pain. A time or two Pecos had to stop and dismount and open gates, and Randall blessed these moments when the jolting stopped, and he wished that the wagon had never to move again. When they did come into Circle-S's yard and Pecos announced their whereabouts, Randall was surprised, for he had lost all track of time and distance. Also, he was fretful. He said weakly, "We've got to catch up with that trail herd."

"Not tonight," Pecos said. "We've got to get us some sleep. And a change of horses."

Getting out of the wagon was even more difficult than climbing in had been. The yard was formless, dark as the inside of a boot; and Randall, realizing that this was the darkness before dawn, knew that Pecos had chosen a slow and careful route homeward. He was mighty grateful to Pecos and tried saying so, but talking required too much effort. He felt Pecos' arm about him and let the old-timer guide him across the yard. At the gallery steps, Randall stumbled. Pecos got him up the steps and into the house and to Dan Saxon's bedroom. . . .

Here Randall must have fainted again, for his next consciousness was of being in the bed, and he discovered that he had been stripped naked. The bed felt good to him; the bed was so pleasurable as to be almost an agony. He burrowed deep into the bed and let its softness cradle him. Presently he heard movement in the house. He listened and judged that Pecos must be somewhere about. He heard voices and listened even harder, wondering who was here with Pecos. He supposed that one of the hands who'd been left with the gathered herd had come to the ranch. He tried to identify that cowpoke's voice; they had become individuals to him this past week, those Circle-S men.

At the moment he realized that it was not a man speaking, Rita came into the bedroom. He couldn't understand this; Rita had gone with the trail herd and should be ten or fifteen miles along the way toward the railroad construction camp. But she was here. She came to the bedside and stood, an indistinct shape in the darkness.

"Where are you hurt?" she asked.

"All over," he said. "My arms and chest mostly."

She seated herself on the edge of the bed and ran her hands under the blankets, and he felt her fingers upon his aching flesh, soft and soothing. She began to manipulate the muscles of his shoulders and arms, her manner as cool and impersonal as a medico's. Her fingers moved constantly, not probing too hard when his wincing indicated that she had touched an especially sore spot. Her fingers had a magic in them that smoothed the sharper edges of pain away and brought him a pleasant lassitude. He asked sleepily, "Where did you learn to do this?" The thing was all a damn' nice dream.

"From a Mexican woman who was my nursemaid when I was a child. My mother's people were Spanish, you know. My mother and father met in Texas; and when my father trailed north, Doña Theresa came along. Her family had served my mother's family for generations. She knew many such tricks at this one, that old Doña Theresa. Many times she eased the soreness of vaqueros who'd been pitched from horses."

Her voice was soft in the darkness, soft as her fingers, and he knew that her talk was part of the ministrations, meant to soothe him. He asked, "Your mother? She passed away?"

Her voice caught. "On that drive north. We met Comanches in the Nations who demanded tribute to let us pass through their territory. Thirty horses, they wanted. My father refused them, and there was a fight. My mother was killed by a Comanche arrow. She is buried on the bank of the Canadian."

"You couldn't have really known her then."

"Not ever. But sometimes when my father talks about her, I feel that I know her."

He said, "I'm sorry." He surrendered himself to the magic of her fingers and was conscious of her nearness and comforted by it. At last his eyes grew heavy, and he was wafted outward to the sweet forgetfulness of sleep.

• CHAPTER 4 •

The High Road

HE AWOKE TO A ROOM GOLDEN WITH SUNLIGHT AND was content to lie in Dan Saxon's bed and enjoy such languid luxury. He was strangely at peace with himself until remembrance came rushing, and he thought of many things then, of Gault Telford's play and Pecos' loyalty and the discovery of his own uselessness when he'd tried to clamber into the wagon. Also, he thought of that trail herd climbing into the hills, all the hopes of Circle-S riding with it, and he bestirred himself and got from the bed. He was stiff in every muscle, but not as stiff as he'd supposed he would be. He remembered Rita's soothing fingers; but that was like a dream remembered, pleasant to contemplate but without reality. He tried walking and found that his legs obeyed him. His clothes were here, tossed carelessly aside when Pecos had stripped him. He got into them.

When he'd latched his gun belt about his waist, he tried a few practice draws. His right arm now moved to his will without pain clamoring through him, but the movement was sluggish, lacking that extra edge of speed that made all the difference. He would have to favor that arm for a long time.

He went out upon the gallery and looked upon the golden morning and at once saw that Pecos' wagon was gone. The ranch had an emptiness to it, the serenity of desertion. He lifted his eyes to the hills and thought of the crew up there, and Pecos hard on their trail. He felt suddenly lonesome; and this for him was a strange feeling, for he had long walked alone, not caring. He saw that smoke lifted from the cook shack, and as he looked that way, Rita framed herself in the shack's doorway and beckoned to him. Lifting his hand to her, he crossed the yard.

"Breakfast is ready," she said.

He washed himself at the basin on the bench, ran a hand over the stubble on his chin and came inside and took a chair. "Pecos got started early?" he asked.

"He thought that grub should get delivered."

He began eating; she served him in that same cool, impersonal manner she had displayed last night. He said, "Thanks for what you did for me."

She turned her back to him and busied herself with the coffee pot. "How do you feel?"

"Able to ride."

She refilled his coffee cup and went outside. When he'd finished eating and walked over to the corrals, he found that she'd saddled two horses. He took up the reins of one and made ready to mount; and then, remembering, he shifted the reins from his left hand to his right, grasped the horn with his left hand, and hauled himself up, making an awkward mount. His back was to Rita and he wasn't sure whether she saw him, but at least she said nothing. They lined out together and rode from the yard.

"This way," she directed.

The spoor of the trail herd was easy to follow; and they moved along the base of the hills, riding stirrup to stirrup for the first few miles. Then they began climbing an old logging road that rose in gentle pitches into the timber and took a tortuous way through the woods. Randall, who'd worked cattle on the open Texas plains, whistled to himself. Here the herd must have been forced down till the cows moved four or five abreast, but at least the palisade of pine on either side of the road had done the work of the flanking riders. He wondered how much time the drive had made on such terrain. Ten miles the first day, he judged. It was now high noon, and he estimated that it would be deep dark before they would come upon the herd. He kept looking ahead for Pecos' wagon; but since they didn't overtake it, he decided that Pecos had indeed got an early start.

The saddle was sheer punishment, but he tried always not to show it. Remembering the wagon's jolting of the night before, he was surprised that the saddle hurt him no more than it did, and again he remembered Rita's fingers. There must have been ancient magic in her ministrations, something handed down from the primitive ones. Later on, when Rita pointed out a shortcut and they left the logging road to follow a narrow game trail across the face of the hillside, he contrived to ride behind her and took secretly to massaging his right arm.

This game trail led them back to the logging road in due course, and in midafternoon they came upon a grassy mountain meadow, cupped high on the hillside, where the drovers had made camp the night before. The sign was plain to read—the black scar where the coosie's fire had been built, the trampled grass where the herd had been bedded, the droppings of the remuda. Randall found the very spot where the chuck-wagon had stood and detected the fresh signs of the passage of Pecos' wagon.

"Well, we made better time than the herd did," he observed.

Rita raised her hand, pointing up the hillside. "Up there," she said.

Randall listened intently, standing in his stirrups and leaning forward. Across the bright, blue sky a hawk wheeled; in the brush a magpie chattered. Somewhere nearby a mountain creek splashed over rocks and made raucous music. Yet in this high, still air he thought that he detected the remote sounds of men and movement, distant and illusive, the faint bawling of cattle, the lifted voices of the drovers. Or was that some fantasy born of expectation? He wasn't sure, and presently he gave up listening and they began riding again.

Darkness overtook them all too soon. There was a brief twilight after the sun had plunged behind the hills, a period when all the world hushed down; and then the trail became a black tunnel. Sometimes as they felt their way along, the timber thinned and the basin lay like a lake of darkness below them, broken by the scattered pinpoints of light that marked the ranches and the distant twinkling cluster that was Sleeping Cat.

Now Randall had to trust to Rita's judgment, but she knew the country well and led the way in a silence that was broken only by her occasional warnings of low-hanging branches or abrupt turns of the trail. They moved onward and upward, and soon Randall heard the bawling of cattle. He tried to orient the sound, but it was a vagrant ghost roaming the night. Then they burst upon another of those mountain meadows and saw a fire burning ahead. Shortly they rode into the circle of its light.

Here stood the high tilts of the chuck wagon, and Pecos' wagon was nearby. Yonder, the bedded herd made a vast blur upon the land; and within the firelight's rim stood Dan Saxon, a two-day's beard stubble showing on his aristocratic face and his hand no longer bandaged—Dan Saxon, and Pecos, and a few of the Circle-S hands who were not otherwise employed. And Curly Mather.

As Rita stepped down from her saddle, Mather said, "Well, I see you found him."

His tone held a truculence which revealed both his anger and his jealousy; and Randall came at once to the ground and stood ready, knowing Mather to be a man whose imaginings had pressed him to the exploding point. He felt sorry for Mather in this moment, sorry that any man should be so prodded as to make such a display of himself. Yet he also felt the full force of Mather's hatred for him.

Rita said, "I'm tired, Curly, and hungry. Whatever you've got to say can keep till later."

"No!" Mather snapped and took a quick step toward her, seizing her arm. "You've made a fool of me, running off to see what was keeping him."

Rita cried, "Let go!" and wrenched free of Mather.

Dan Saxon's face had hardened, and he moved toward Mather. Randall said, his voice like a whiplash, "That's enough, Curly!" He faced Mather, remembering then that he could not stand up against Mather either with fist or gun, not since last night. There was a long-drawn-out moment when the two stood with eyes locked, flint and stone striking sparks. For the space of a watch tick, Randall was sure Mather would come at him. The wild intent was naked on his face. Then Mather dropped his eyes and turned and strode off into the darkness.

Randall shrugged. "Where's the coosie?" he demanded. "I'm hungry." But he was thinking, Sooner or later he'll find out I've been cut into the culls!

He got a plate from the cook and ate his supper; shortly after that he rolled into a blanket upon the ground. The fire died, and others bedded near him. He found Rita's tarp next to his own, and after an hour she came to him silently, and he felt her fingers probing at him and working last night's magic, that ancient art that had been born in Mexico and come from there to Texas and thence to Montana. Again he was soothed to sleep, having time only to grin wryly with the thought that Curly Mather ought to see them now!

In the morning there was all the confusion of getting the trail herd underway again, but before full daylight they were wending onward, Mather riding in point position and the chuck wagon jolting far ahead. There was a day of this, and another and another; and one of those days they made only five miles, for the country grew wilder and more rugged, and sometimes the trail was a mere thread through the wilderness, and sometimes there was no trail at all.

By night they bedded the herd and guarded it through the long watches, the old songs of the nighthawks lifting in the darkness. By day they fought the mountain's pitch and the mountain's many faces. Always Mather kept apart from Randall now, speaking only when he needed to, and always Randall watched himself, not wanting to betray to any of them that he had returned something less than a whole man. The effects of his beating were wearing off with the passing days, but still the saddle punished him; and when he tried his gun arm in his secret moments, he found improvement in his speed but was far from satisfied.

Then, on the third day after he had rejoined the herd, Dan Saxon lifted his hand in the stillness of the afternoon; and when the others strained their ears at this signal, they also heard what Saxon had heard, the distant mournful, hoot of a locomotive in these high reaches. Thereafter, Saxon rode on ahead of the herd; and when the night camp was made, he returned jubilant.

"The rails have been moving, too," he reported. "The construction camp is nearer than it was when I first made the dicker. We'll have this beef delivered by tomorrow afternoon."

The men were a beaten bunch, worn thin by the arduous uphill trail, but they stirred to life with the news and even raised a ragged cheer. The cook spread a treat for supper, a row of dried-apple pies, each with Circle-S's brand cut into the crust. Randall looked about him at the drawn, bearded faces; and sharing their tiredness and their jubilation, he was one with his crew.

Afterwards Rita wandered off afoot in the darkness. Randall saw her go, and on impulse he moved after her. She had found a trail that wove through the timber, and he followed along this trail until it came upon a high, rocky ledge that overlooked the basin. Now the lights of Sleeping Cat were far more remote than they had been that first night he and Rita had climbed the high road. Rita stood here in the starlight, her back to him, looking upon the panorama below. He came behind her and said softly, "Rita?"

"Yes?" she said, not turning.

He had had little communication with her since they'd joined the drive. He had followed her tonight with no intent that he could have named, but now he slipped his arms around her, and she turned within the circle of his arms and faced him. He looked at her in the starlight and saw her sultry sadness; he looked at those full lips so rich in promise. He smiled then, knowing why he had come. He said softly, "Do you know, that first night I thought you'd stayed at the ranch instead of going along with the drive. I didn't know until Curly spoke up that you'd turned back to find me."

She looked away from him. "The grub was important to the drive. We all began to worry when you and Pecos didn't join us on the trail."

She was keeping her voice even, and he knew she was trying to imply that it hadn't been for him that she'd turned back. But he also knew her calm was costing her an effort. And he was conscious of her suppleness within his arms, conscious that she wasn't moving away from him. He tightened his arms around her and drew her close, and his lips went seeking hers. For a moment she fought against him, turning her face aside, and then her lips were on his. Her arms closed about him and her fingers strayed to the nape of his neck. For a long moment they were thus, and then she was pushing him away.

"No!" she cried.

"Rita! Rita!" he murmured, not understanding.

"Tomorrow it's all over. This isn't just a way for me to stay on Circle-S. And that's what you'd come to think some day."

He put his hands to her shoulders and held her at arm's length. "You're wrong. You're so very wrong."

Then he heard the faint stirring in the timber behind him, and the alarm on her face told him that she had heard, too. He wheeled about, placing himself between her and whatever moved in the brush; and he got his gun out and stood with it in his hand, keening the darkness. He heard the sound again, fainter this time. He cried; "Who's there?"

But there was only silence; no answer came back to him but the empty echo of his voice.

They made ready to move the herd in the darkness before dawn, and Dan Saxon came to Randall in the midst of all the confusion. "Curly's gone," Saxon reported.

Randall had just taken the early morning kinks out of his horse. He dismounted after the fashion of a roper, leaping from his saddle so that he wouldn't have to lower himself by the use of his arm. "Yes?" he asked.

"I didn't miss him last night," Saxon said. "But I've asked a few questions this morning. Curly took a walk right after supper. He came back shortly, looking as black as any thundercloud, so the boys tell me. He cut his private saddler out of the remuda and rode off without a word."

Randall fashioned up a cigarette, his mind harking back to the night before, and he knew now who had made movement in the brush when he'd been holding Rita in his arms on the rocky ledge yonder. Mather had followed them and spied upon them, and then Mather had quit the drive. Randall and Rita had come back to the camp at once and gone directly to their soogans, and it had been Randall's judgment at the time that some animal had prowled the brush. Now he knew differently. He turned the knowledge over in his mind and was sorry for Mather. The man had had his own kind of strength and savvy, but it hadn't been enough.

"He's got some pay due him," Randall said.

"I'll know where to find him when the time comes," Saxon said and turned away.

Randall watched him go. Saxon hadn't shaved since leaving the ranch, and his beard, gray-shot and inclined to curl, gave him a peculiar dignity. Moreover, it hid his mouth and made him a harder man to read than before. He had given his report on Mather with no more concern than if he had mentioned a limping horse or some other small nuisance of the day. Yet the feeling was in Randall that Saxon had anticipated Mather's desertion. It was as though all men were to Saxon the cards in a deck, as though Saxon, the gambler always, had judged Mather's worth and had expected what would come when the deck was shuffled. Once Randall had had the feeling that Dan Saxon was unbeatable. How could you jar a man who always knew how the cards would fall?

Thinking this, Randall remembered Telford's claim—that a gambling debt couldn't be legally collected. Yet Saxon had been ready to remove himself from Circle-S the morning Randall had ridden out to take over. Had that been a bluff on Saxon's part? Come to reflect on it, Saxon might even be playing *him* like a card! Yet he believed not.

Rope ends were popping, and riders made movement in the chilly murk. Already the chuck wagon was lumbering along ahead, and the herd was being shaped up and pointed on its way. Shrugging, Randall put out his quirly, rose to saddle and went to work. A man made his choices; Curly Mather had made his. But Randall was remembering Rita pushing him, Randall, away last night and crying, "Tomorrow it's all over . . ." Mather's chance had been the strong chance, but he hadn't waited to learn that. With a cut of the cards, Long Tom Randall had won everything—save Rita! Now why hadn't Mather savvied that?

They began moving the herd along, and the morning came strong and clear, sunlight dispelling the chill of the high country dawn. The cattle were strung out through the pine; they moved across the face of the hill; they moved toward the sky. Randall looked for Rita and saw her riding in swing position. He was at drag, and there were bunch-quitters to keep him busy. He thought he recognized that old mossyhorn that had charged him his first day in the saddle for Circle-S. He laid the end of his rope across the mossyhorn's rump. "Now how in hell did you get cut into the prime beef?" he demanded.

He watched Rita whenever he was free enough to do so. He hoped she would ride back and join him, but she kept her distance, and he knew that she wished it that way. Once she'd spoken to him of pride, and now he knew how strong hers was. He was remembering her saying, "This isn't just a way for me to stay on Circle-S. And that's what you'd come to think some day."

He had been a selfish man, keeping his eyes always on his own ambition, trailing long spurs wherever he walked. From the first, he had supposed that Rita was as selfish. Now he thought about last night and was perplexed and a little angry, for he had come up against something beyond his experience and understanding. He felt the way he had that day he'd dug the arrowhead from the ranchhouse shutter and flung it away, not knowing why he'd done so.

The mournful wail of a locomotive drifted over the hills again, the sound seeming to be almost in their midst. Soon Randall made out the chuffing of a work train, the beat of hammers against spikes, the clanging of rails being lowered into place. Men's voices reached him in tattered, meaningless fragments. These sounds haunted the mountain air. Circle-S's crew quickened and began moving the cattle a bit faster, and Circle-S's crew took to smiling.

Just past noon they broke out of timber, and in the openness before them they saw their destination. Across the shoulder of the hill ran the yellow welt of the grade, loose ties piled beside it. Teamsters were shouting at work horses; this sound blended with the clanging sledges and the hissing of steam from a locomotive. Weather-beaten tents and construction shacks were scattered upon the flat, a makeshift town. Men were everywhere, swarming about like ants. And the Circle-S herd, spilling from the pine, advanced upon them, advanced upon end of steel.

The chuck wagon up front did not stop for the preparation of a noonday meal. Circle-S would eat at tables in the commissary shack today. They drove on, their hunger forgotten; and shortly Dan Saxon, riding point position, made the circling movement of his hand that signaled for the herd to be milled and bedded, and then Saxon and Randall rode into the construction camp.

They were looking for the grading contractor who would buy the beef, and at long last they found him in a crude shack where a telegraph instrument clattered, a stoop-shouldered operator hunched over it. The contractor was a big man with a hearty voice, and he gave his hand to Saxon and then was introduced to Randall. "One of my foremen has already looked over the beef and reported to me," he told Saxon. "It's fine looking stuff."

Saxon said, "You will pay Mr. Randall. And you can talk to him about future deliveries. He's the new owner of Circle-S."

The contractor frowned. "There's a hitch."

"A hitch?"

The contractor tipped his head toward the telegraph instrument. "A wire came this morning from the sheriff at the county seat. He ordered the cash impounded that I was to have paid you for the beef. The money is to go to a Mr. Gault Telford of Sleeping Cat to meet notes he holds against Circle-S. Notes now overdue."

Dan Saxon said very quietly, "Those notes are not due for another sixty days."

The contractor waved an arm. "That's something you'll have to settle with this fellow Telford. I can't be involved in personal squabbles. Neither can I go bucking local law, if I want to get this spur finished. I'll take the beef if you're willing to leave it. I've got hungry men to feed. But you'll have to straighten out that matter of the money before I can turn it over to you."

Randall said, "Keep the beef."

He turned then and walked from the shack. It came to him that he was very tired and that the work of the fists of Telford's plug-uglies was still taking its toll. He walked along in the strong sunlight; he walked through all the chaos of the construction camp with no conscious thought. Men brushed by him, and once the wheel of a freight wagon narrowly missed him, and he was roundly cursed by the teamster for his carelessness. He gave the teamster an unsmiling look, not really hearing the man.

He walked until he came to a frame-and-canvas structure that bore the crude legend: SALOON. Into this he turned and found a sawdust-strewn floor and a plank bar. Silence and coolness were here, and only the bartender was inside at this hour. From him Randall ordered whiskey. He downed the drink fast and felt it warm him, and he ordered again but left the second drink untouched for a long time.

All his thinking was wooden, and at the core of it was a numb sort of hatred for Gault Telford. Overdue notes! A flick of the pen would have changed the dates, and Telford himself would probably have that sort of skill. Telford had planned this little sandy from the first, timing it so the sheriff would have his piece spoken over the railroad telegraph before the beef got to the camp. Once he, Randall, had expected a raid on Circle-S and he'd stood alert and ready for that raid. Then he'd supposed that Telford had satisfied himself with the beating that his men had inflicted. But the Telfords played a different kind of game, and the beating had only been part of it. The beating was to have kept Long Tom Randall from retaliating when the real play was made, retaliating with a call for a showdown with a fast gun.

* * *

Randall downed his second drink and ordered a third. He was hungry, he realized, and he thought to find the crew and join them at table. He owed the crew wages, he recalled; he was a ranch-owner now. Well, there was enough money left in that Denver bank to take care of them. He began to laugh then, thinking how he had finished out a circle. He would go back to Texas busted flat, back to being another forty-a-month cowpoke.

"Easy come, easy go," he said aloud.

The bartender said sympathetically, "You look like a man with things on your mind, friend."

"Yes," Randall said, "I am thinking about killing a man. I am thinking about killing him because there is no other way his kind can be stopped. How do you outsmart a spider? You don't. You tear his web from its dusty corner and stamp the whole business, spider and all, under your heel. That's the way you fix a spider. Isn't it so?"

The bartender looked startled. Then he said soothingly, "Have one on the house. No use being in a hurry about that killing. It can wait until tomorrow."

Randall took the drink that was slid across the bar to him. "Sure, it can wait."

He bought a drink for himself and one for the bartender. He decided that the bartender was a very understanding man, a good man to be with when the maggots were crawling in a man's brain and he faced his own defeat and didn't like the looks of it. He had still another drink. Come to think of it, what sense was there in killing Telford? They only put a rope around your neck for that kind of cavorting, so in the end you were just as dead as Telford. No, he'd been licked, and he might just as well tuck his tail between his legs and skulk back to Texas.

"Tomorrow it's all over," Rita had said. How right she'd been!

"You're laughing," the barkeep said. "It's good for a man to laugh. Drink up!"

He heard Rita then. She was crying, "Tom!"

He turned very slowly, keeping one elbow on the bar because he liked the solid feel of it. He saw her in the doorway of the saloon, and his muddled thought was that this was a hell of a place for her to be.

She came toward him and said, "I've been looking all over for you!"

"And now you've found me," he said.

"It's dad. He's gone!"

"He's down at the telegraph shack."

"No, he left there more than an hour ago. They tell me he took a fresh horse and headed out." Her hand closed on his arm and he saw how agitated she was. "Tom, I think he's gone looking for Gault Telford. I talked to the contractor. Dad told him he intended to make Telford admit those notes were doctored."

He was a nearly sober man then; it was as though icy water had been flung on him. He said, "That's my job! If anybody braces Telford, it's going to be me!"

She said, "But your gun arm's no good. Don't you think I saw how you mounted your horse that first day? And I've watched you since. You're in no shape for fighting!"

He laid his hands on her shoulders, gripping her hard. "Dan Saxon knew that, too?" he demanded.

"Yes. I told him."

He was suddenly completely sober. He said, "His own hand isn't much more than healed. The damn' fool! Doesn't he know Telford will be expecting one of us to come rampaging?" He released her and started for the door.

Rita cried, "Where are you going?"

"After him!" he flung back.

• Chapter 5 •
Hard Rider

HE HAD LEFT HIS HORSE TIED BEFORE THE TELEGRAPH shack; and when he got the mount and rode out to the herd, he found only Pecos and the cook. These two were holding the herd while the rest of the crew had gone into the construction camp to eat and watch the fascinating business of a railroad being built. To Pecos, Randall said, "Look over the remuda and cut me out the fastest saddler that packs Circle-S's brand."

Pecos squinted at him. "Dan got that cayuse over an hour ago. You'll have to take second best."

"Then get leather on it!"

Pecos said, "Now why is everybody in such an all-fired rush?"

"Rita can tell you about it," Randall said impatiently. "I've got to get riding. Cook, throw a little grub into a saddlebag."

Randall helped with the saddling, after Pecos had found him a leggy roan that looked as thought it might be both fast and long on bottom. Randall, clumsy with the kak, made no effort to hide his awkwardness. Pecos knew his secret anyway, and the time for pretense had passed. This was the time for action. Now why in hell had Dan Saxon, that most careful of men, gone off half-cocked?

Randall lifted himself to leather, snatched up the saddlebag the cook had prepared for him, waved his hand at Pecos and lined out for the timber. And thus he began the hardest ride of his life.

For the first few miles, backtracking over the trail the herd had taken, he rode as recklessly as the terrain permitted, spurred by a feverish urgency. Time and again he risked himself and the horse on rocky slopes, heedless of anything but the need to lop off the miles. He tried to remember exactly how far it was to Circle-S; he recalled each day of the drive and the campfire talk when the crew had estimated how much ground had been covered. Five miles some days, ten miles at the most. He decided that it must be between thirty and forty miles to the ranch and wondered if he could make it to Circle-S before deep dark came down. After the first hour, he realized how futile was such a hope. There were too many places where the horse had to pick its way through brush and shale and deadfall.

But always Randall pushed onward and downward, growing angry when the pace had to be slow. Sky and timber and rocky trail became an endlessness never changing; he had the feeling that he rode a treadmill, taking toll of himself and the horse, getting nowhere. When he got occasional glimpses of the basin below, he was tempted to find his own trail, remembering the shortcut Rita had taken on the way up. But his only real knowledge of the hill country was over the route the herd had followed. He fought down his impatience, knowing that any deviation from the route might only slow him.

Sometimes he saw remembered landmarks from the trip upward—a lightning-blasted pine tree, a rock shaped like a beaver's head, a grassy meadow where the coosie had hauled his chuck wagon to a stop and doled out coffee. These were cheering sights; they made milestones of a sort and lessened the feeling that he was treadmilling. But when the sun dropped behind the hills, he felt that time was slipping away from him. After the brief twilight, he had to slow to a walk, even on the levels, for darkness claimed all the country. He rode with an elbow crooked before his face, wary of branches.

For an hour and another he groped his way along, and then he faced the inevitable. In one of those grassy meadows where a mountain creek brawled, he stripped gear from the horse and led the mount back and forth, gradually cooling it off and permitting it to drink sparingly. After that he improvised a squaw-hobble from a gunnysack he'd picked up along the trail, ate the food from the saddlebag, and stretched himself upon the blanket.

His thoughts ran riot; and when he half-slumbered, he had the sensation of being back in the saddle and riding hard. In his wakeful moments he shaped up cigarette after cigarette and lay with his head pillowed on his clasped hands, looking at the sky above and hoping that Saxon, likewise, had decided to quit riding till dawn. He wondered where in the darkness and the hills Saxon was bedded. A mile away? Five miles? Ten?

He knew now what had driven Saxon. Today had been like that day Saxon had braced him, shortly after he'd stepped from the stagecoach in Sleeping Cat. Saxon played all his cards carefully, but there always came those reckless moments when a last chip had to be tossed upon the table. Telford's trickery had made another such moment. Saxon had reasoned as he, Randall, had reasoned in the construction camp saloon. There was now only one answer to Telford. But the thing that was beyond Randall's understanding, and stood now between him and sleep was the constant question: why must Saxon fight Circle-S's fight?

He turned this over in his mind until exhaustion claimed him and he slept. He was up with the first show of light and into the saddle again, tightening his belt against hunger's clamor. He wished he'd got more grub from the coosie, but he set his mind against hunger and pushed the horse hard. His thought was that if Saxon hadn't stopped last night he might be almost to Sleeping Cat by now, and the thought made Randall reckless again. He rode the horse until the animal began to heave under him. Realizing he must ration the horse's strength for all the miles that remained, he gave the mount respite.

The sun was not very high when he came to the meadow where Circle-S had made its camp the first night of the drive. After that he tried looking for the place where the game trail he and Rita had taken rejoined the old logging road, but he couldn't be sure. From the promontories he looked down upon a jungle of pine tops, and the sight of all that timber told him he'd best stay with the road. In midmorning he reached the bottom of the hill and could now skirt along level ground to Circle-S. He lifted his flagging horse to a high gallop and held it there; he gritted his teeth against the punishment of the saddle, and shortly before noon he rode into Circle-S's empty yard.

Smoke lifted from the cook shack, and at Randall's shout one of the cowhands who'd stayed behind to guard the roundup gather showed himself.

"Dan Saxon here?"

"Changed horses and rode toward town about twenty minutes ago."

Relief left Randall weak. So Saxon hadn't pushed on through the night, not if he were only such a short ways ahead! Randall came down from the saddle and almost fell. He looked at the sweat- and foam-mottled horse that had served him and was sorry for the horse, sorry he'd had to ask so much of it. "Lead this cayuse till he cools off," he ordered the man. "And saddle me a fast hide."

While the man went to do his bidding, Randall lurched toward the cook shack. He knew he should be making the minutes count now, but he also knew he would have to eat if he were to stick a saddle to Sleeping Cat. He came inside to find the huge coffee pot simmering on the stove. There was food in a frying pan shoved back from the heat—the dinner of the man who was now taking care of the horse. This food Randall wolfed down and followed it with two cups of coffee. He even stole time for the luxury of a cigarette, and then he came out of the cook shack.

The Circle-S hand was still leading the spent horse back and forth, but a saddled horse stood ready and waiting. Randall hauled himself into the saddle, using his right hand on the horn. Mounted, he realized that though old habit had dictated his move, his arm hadn't failed him. His arm was still stiff, but it had supported his weight.

"I ate your dinner," he shouted at the Circle-S man. "I'll cook you one when I get back."

Then he was away again, a fresh horse under him and food in his belly and a feeling running through him that he could lick the world. He was upon familiar terrain he had traveled twice, but he had to remember that Saxon was now nearly an hour ahead of him. His first exuberance wore off with that thought, the old fretful impatience returning. He resented the gates that had to be opened; but true to rangeland tradition, he carefully closed them. Soon he was beyond Circle-S's graze and lining out for Sleeping Cat.

Plying quirt and spur, he thundered along, the land blurring beneath him and the breeze of his own making a hard hand against him. He peered ahead, trying to sight Saxon's dust, but there was just enough rise and fall to the land to limit visibility. In midafternoon, he sighted Sleeping Cat and thereafter kept his eyes on the town whenever he could, watching the scatteration of buildings grow within his vision. But Sleeping Cat's nearness was still an illusion made of high, thin air and strong sunshine, and it was late afternoon before he rode into the outskirts.

That was when he heard the guns.

The sound came from somewhere up the street—one shot, and another on the heels of it, the false fronts catching the thunder and echoing it. In Randall then was one sickening thought: too late! He flogged the horse onward and came into the familiar main street; and the scene was as he'd anticipated it, the two rows of buildings and the horses at hitch rails and the loiterers withdrawn at the smell of trouble to peep furtively from doorways. Before the hotel, he saw Dan Saxon standing in almost the precise spot he'd stood that evening he'd braced Randall. The man was erect, a smoking gun in his hand, and across the way Gault Telford lay crumpled in the dust of the street, a gun, fallen from his hand, before him.

Randall flung himself off his horse. "Dan!" he called.

Saxon turned his head slowly and looked at Randall, but Dan's real attention was elsewhere. "Watch out, Tom!" he shouted.

A bullet drove at Randall, tugging at the brim of his sombrero. Instinctively he crouched, his hand dropping to his holster. Another bullet kicked dust at his feet, but now his sluggish arm obeyed him and he got his gun into his hand. He saw Curly Mather then; Mather had come around the corner of the stage depot to stand under its eave. Hammering a shot, Randall saw Mather double over and fall on his face. All this happened too quickly for conscious thought; then Randall remembered Saxon saying of Curly Mather the morning

Mather had deserted, "I'll know where to find him when the time comes."

How well Saxon had known! There was an inevitability here, the inevitability that Mather, rejecting Circle-S in his blind hate and jealousy, would go straight to Telford to cast his lot with Telford.

Randall thought, He knew! At the last he knew about my gun arm, for Telford told him. That was why he got bold enough.

Walking over to Telford's sprawled body, he looked down at Telford and knew for a moment a surging resentment against Dan Saxon. Randall had hated no man so much as he had hated Gault Telford. Yet his hate was less than two weeks old, and Saxon's had been forged across many years. Remembering this, he saw that this day and this hour had been Saxon's due, and the resentment was gone. Kneeling, he turned Telford over and explored the man's pockets till he found Telford's wallet. He turned and looked at Saxon, who still stood unmoving, for all the world like an actor taking his curtain call.

Randall said, "The notes are here. He didn't even bother to change the dates. He just told his lie to the sheriff and made it stick."

Saxon said woodenly, "I laid my tongue on him, goaded him into drawing first, just as I goaded you that night. I've learned a little bit about trickery myself."

Randall looked quickly about. "There were four men—"

Saxon nodded toward the far end of the street where a distant dust cloud marked the passage of horsemen out of Sleeping Cat. "I got Telford alone when I braced him. Those others hit the saddle as soon as he fell. That's the trouble with some hired men. They stick only as long as the paymaster is around."

Randall said, "It's all done then." He came toward Saxon and stood before the man. Saxon smiled a slow smile and let the gun slip from his fingers, then pitched forward into Randall's arms. The man was white as a sheet.

Catching him, Randall cried, "You're hit!"

"My shoulder. I've lost blood. I'll be all right."

"Where's the doctor?"

"Down the street."

Randall led Saxon along, supporting him. They got to the picket fence around Doc Farrell's place, and Saxon said, "I can make it inside. He'll bed me for the night. I'll see you at Circle-S in the morning."

Randall hesitated a moment. "Just one thing. I've got to know why in hell you did it."

Saxon said, "I thought you knew. You were told once that the Saxons don't cheat. You had a clear ranch coming to you. That made it my chore. Now do you understand?"

"Yes," Randall said. "I understand everything."

• Chapter 6 •
A Man's Iron

LIGHT GLOWED IN CIRCLE-S'S RANCHHOUSE WHEN Randall rode into the yard; and this surprised him, for the hour was late. He had taken a slow way home from Sleeping Cat, sparing himself and sparing the horse, for all the accumulated hours and miles had weighed heavily upon him. He had done much thinking on this return journey; he had grown weary of thinking. When he saw the light, he supposed that one of the Circle-S hands who'd been left here was in the house.

He rode to the corral and dismounted and began hauling gear from the horse. He was at this when a lantern bobbed across the yard as someone came from the house toward him. It was Rita.

She held the lantern high and looked at him. She said, "I rode down as fast as I could. I knew that if either of you was able to come back, you'd come here."

He saw how very tired she looked; yet she was composed; she was ready for all the inevitabilities. Knowing this, he sought quick words to spare her the question she hadn't yet asked.

"Your dad got scratched," he said. "I left him at Doc Farrell's. He'll be home tomorrow. Telford's dead. I have the notes, and we can collect as soon as I show that railroad contractor that Telford was lying." He paused. "Curly's dead, too. He bought in."

He wasn't sure how she would take this last news. It hit her; he could see that. But when she did speak, her voice was even. "He was a suspicious man," she said. "All of our lives it would have been the same—his spying on ever move I made and twisting what he saw to his own imaginings. I was sorry for him when he was alive. I am sorry that he is dead."

Randall finished with the horse and walked back toward the ranchhouse. She came along with him, the lantern in her hand and their shadows scissoring in its light. She climbed to the gallery, but here he lagged behind her. From the foot of the steps, he said, "I'll be sleeping in the bunkhouse."

She placed the lantern on the porch and seated herself on the top step, drawing her knees up under her chin and folding her arms about her knees. "Just for tonight?"

"From here on out, Rita. The house belongs to Dan Saxon, the man who built it. So does the ranch. I'll talk to him when he gets back. I've got a little money in Denver. Maybe he'd let me buy into this ranch. I think we'd make a good pair of partners."

She shook her head. "The Saxons pay their gambling debts. What about that?"

"I want only what I've really won," he said.

She drew in a quick breath; her face was suddenly alive with a strange expectancy. "I've seen you change," she said. "I didn't know you'd changed so much. Why, Tom?"

He seated himself on the lowest step. He was a somber man still wrestling with the truths that had come to him. "Remember, you said that some day someone would bring me to my knees?"

"Curly? At the end?"

"No. Dan Saxon."

Again she shook her head. "I'm afraid I don't understand."

He said, "I told you once that I figured I was born too late, born into a rigged world where those who'd had the easy pickings years ago could keep a hard bit in the mouths of men like me. Then I got my chance at ownership. I sweated the first day I rode out here, and I should have learned from that what ownership meant—sweating and taking responsibility, like I had to take when my crew was low on grub. But there was even more that I didn't savvy, the constant standing guard a man had to do to hold what had come to him, first against Indians and rustlers and then against Gault Telford. Your father tried to tell me about that, but I was too concerned with what Long Tom Randall wanted. I didn't hear him."

She said softly, "No man could have told you the things you had to learn."

He nodded. "No part of it was free, not for Dan or any other man. I know that now. He buried a wife in the Nations, and that was part of the price. He kept paying across all the years in one way or another. He was paying at the last, when he rode to Sleeping Cat to brace Telford. He did that because he wanted to hand Circle-S over to me clean. That was part of ownership, too, the part I was slowest to understand—the pride a man has to have in his own iron. Some day, when I've lived enough years and soaked enough of my sweat into this ground, I'll be able to feel that kind of pride. It would be an empty thing, just winning ownership by a cut of the cards."

"Yes," she said, "it would be. Just as it would have been an empty thing for me to stay here if the thought had ever struck you that my staying was only a cheap bargain. That was what I was trying to tell you the other night in the hills. A woman has her kind of pride of ownership, too.''

He sat silent for a long moment, thinking of the things said and the things unsaid. He remembered how it had been that first day he'd ridden on roundup and found a pride in an old skill. He flexed his right arm. He supposed that arm might never have its old quickness. A legend would die, and he was glad of its passing. Being a legend had meant being lonely. He thought of Pecos and the others; he thought of the cook's row of pies, all bearing Circle-S's brand. He thought how it had been to belong to the crew. He said then, ''Do you think I can make a deal with your father to buy in?''

She said, ''I think that dad would do anything in the world to keep you here. It may sound queer, but I think that from the very first it was Long Tom Randall he hoped to save, even more than he wanted to save the ranch. He was a wild one, my father, long, long ago.'' She smiled at him. ''And what kind of deal have you got to offer me?''

He smiled, too. ''At the end of a day's work, if I'm not too dead beat out, will the boss' beautiful daughter maybe go riding with me?''

She said, ''Did you ever wonder what it was that Curly saw from the very first that made him hate you so much?''

He turned this over in his mind until its full meaning struck him; and when it did, he knew she was near as the reach of his arms. But first he stood up and picked the lantern from the gallery. He walked into the yard with it, bending low and holding the light close to the ground. He searched for many minutes, and finally he picked up an object and came back to the gallery with it. He showed Rita the flint arrowhead he'd once thrown away.

He walked to the shutter from which he'd removed the arrowhead and used his gun-barrel to drive the arrowhead back into place. He said then, "That's to keep me reminded always of what I learned from Dan Saxon."

He opened his arms to her and crossed the short distance between them. She had come to her feet and was awaiting him; he took her into his arms and held her close and began laughing, not with merriment but with the full taste of a freedom he had never known before. She laughed with him, sharing his joy. . . .